S0-AYG-896

TWO MOONS RISING

This book is a work of fiction. The characters, places, incidents, and dialogue are the product of the author's imagination and are not to be construed as real, or if real, are used fictitiously. Any resemblance to actual events, locales, or persons, either living or dead, is purely coincidental.

Copyright © 2015 by Ernest Solar

All rights reserved. No part of this book may be used or reproduced in any manner whatsoever without the prior written permission of the publisher, except in the case of brief quotations embodied in critical articles and reviews.

For more information, to inquire about rights to this or other works, or to purchase copies for special educational, business, or sales promotional uses please write to:

The Zharmae Publishing Press, L.L.C.
5638 Lake Murray Blvd, Suite 217
La Mesa, California 91942
www.zharmae.com

FIRST EDITION

Published in Print and Digital formats in the United States of America

The golden Z logo, and the TZPP logo are trademarks of The Zharmae Publishing Press, L.L.C.

ISBN: 978-1-943549-12-2

Two Moons Rising

Ernest Solar

Barbara,
I hope you always enjoy your dreams!
E Solar 9/3/2015

Seattle | San Diego | Los Angeles

To my Muse, Christine

Two Moons Rising

Prologue

Southern Italy in 1110

The caretaker of the cemetery stepped out of the dark crypt and threw the oil-soaked torch into a bucket by the entrance. The flame of the torch hissed in protest as it extinguished in the cold liquid. He pulled his dark cloak around his chest tighter and wondered if it was colder outside or in the crypt. He glanced up at the fading sunlight in the western sky and then grabbed the inside handle of the heavy iron door and started to tug. In his youth, closing crypt doors was a much easier task, but after forty years it took more effort to accomplish the feat. He grunted and pulled and pushed until the door slowly started to move. He pressed his back against the outside of the door and used the strength of his legs to push the door closed and seal the entrance to the crypt. He secured the entrance with a heavy lock and stepped back to admire his handiwork. He spat on the name plaque of the deceased man in the tomb and walked off.

Book I

I

Research Notes of Dr. James Mac

Journal Entry #17 translated from the "wall" text found in the tomb of Gavin Arbitor, circa 1110

I know not this place. This place with the purple sun. Does it exist in my dreams or in my waking life? I know not. I journey here often. At times under my own free volition or forced into service by our One Almighty God.

I write this for all who find their way here through God's will. The terrain of this place is void of any semblance of trees or bushes from our own. Therefore, this is foreign land to my eyes. Nevertheless, thine eyes still recognize the similarities of our world. The only vegetation recognizable to our kind is the golden stalks of grass that sway in a forceful wind that I have determined blows from the Northern Hemisphere. The calm and silent oceans in the Southern Hemisphere are an emerald green and the waves drift across the surface of the water in eerie silence. The barren terrain with the rolling hills of golden stalks links the mountains of the north to the seas in the south.

As far as I can tell, no living creature inhabits this land. Albeit, life does dwell in this land. Life I have never seen in my own land. Life different from my own appearance. Similar to us in structure. Different than life I have ever experienced in my years. They move and change in ways unbeknownst to my most vivid imagination. Be them demons I think not, for I feel their souls. I feel their souls in this land and recognize their souls among our kind, hidden in the corporeal flesh of our family, friends, and neighbors. Hellions they are not, nonetheless life unknown to our kind filled with an intent to remove us.

Forgive me Lord Almighty for the actions I perform when I journey to this place. Forgive me for the violence that is forced upon my soul in order to protect my own kind from this life that threatens to shroud our very place in your universe. Please, Lord, grant me the strength to be your liberator among our people.

II

A shapeless silver entity, coined the Myst by men long-dead, drifts from the coldness of space to descend through the Earth's atmosphere unnoticed. As the Myst descends through the heavens of the Earth it leisurely floats around and between white threads of light that are invisible to the physical eye. The threads of light crisscross the sky from all different angles with no visible pattern to their movements. As the silver Myst passes each thread of light, a small portion of the entity brushes against the white threads as if touching each one. But the Myst never lingers on one thread for longer than a moment. It acts as if it is looking for one thread in particular. As it descends the upper atmosphere through the clouds, a wisp of the Myst touches a thread and pauses, then wraps itself around the single white thread and travels down the length of it to a rooftop of a brick home in a quiet suburban neighborhood.

The silver Myst untangles itself from the thread and pools at the base of it on the roof. Gradually, a pair of three-fingered hands form in the Myst and grip the thread and start to pull. At first the thread does not move. The Myst hands form forearms and arms and pull harder, and the thread gives way to the added strength of the Myst and moves. Methodically and slowly the Myst pulls and tugs on the white thread until it makes visible progress in its effort. Eventually, on the rooftop of the suburban home, a white shadow of a human form appears on the other end of the thread. The white shadow holds its end of the thread and resists against the force of the Myst, but is unsuccessful in stopping the slow progress. To the human eye, it would appear as if the white shadow and the silver Myst were playing a game of tug-of-war on the roof of the house—a war for that human soul.

The Myst continues to pull and tug on the soul-thread and drag the human soul closer. The Myst forms a head and shoulders to its hands and arms when the human soul is a foot from it. Still holding the soul thread, the Myst floats the rest of the distance to meet the captured soul. Hovering a few feet above the rooftop, the Myst tilts its head from side to side as if to examine the shape and size of the soul. A thin smile stretches across the Myst's thin lips as it recognizes the fear radiating from the human soul. The indistinct shape of the Myst blurs and gradually mimics the shape and size of the captured soul. Then it raises the soul thread that it still holds in its hands and without ceremony severs the thread with a sharp claw.

The soul's face registers a mixture of shock and sorrow and then its white light dissolves into the darkness of night. The Myst examines the severed end of the thread and pushes it into its stomach. A look of ecstasy splashes across the Myst's face before it floats through the roof to enter its new human host.

III

Lance sat in the chairs by the pharmacy in the supermarket and watched the young boy tugging on his mom's sleeve to get her attention. The boy's mother ignored her son as she tried to ask the pharmacist a question. The boy glanced over at Lance and they briefly made eye contact. The boy stopped his tugging and hid behind his mother's legs. Lance smiled and remembered when he was seven years old. He leaned his head back against the wall behind him and closed his eyes just as he did when he and his mother were sitting in the waiting room waiting to see the doctor.

He had promised his mother he would try to stay awake for the doctor's appointment he had in twenty minutes, but the urge to sleep was too great. Lance thought nothing of his sleeping habits. He thought it was normal that this was the third time in four hours that he had fallen asleep. However, his mother thought differently.

With his head on his mother's shoulder, he heard the nurse come into the waiting room and call his name. He tried to open his eyes to stand up and walk, but anyone watching him just saw a little boy continuing to sleep against his mother's arm. Lance mentally tried to give himself a pep talk to try and wake up and move. He could feel his mother shaking him and another female voice calling his name. He wanted to move, but he felt paralyzed in place. Mentally, Lance shrugged his shoulders and quit fighting the resistance to sleep. He kept his eyes closed and let his dreams take him away.

***

Lance stood in the middle of a field of golden grass stalks that stretched upward toward his waist. He knelt down and pulled a stalk of grass toward him and looked at it more closely. The grass was a brownish-gold and felt soft like the fur of a puppy dog. He smiled and aimlessly petted the grass as he looked up toward the sky and the purple sun and silver clouds. Then he looked down at the ground and saw that he was floating a few inches above the soil. He reached down with his hand to try to touch the ground but felt an air bubble push back toward his hand. He pushed harder and the force of the effort propelled him backward through the grass. He stood from his kneeling position and tried to take a step but slid through the air and between the grasses. He smiled and took long bounding leaps through the field, laughing each time as his body floated through the air. He could not remember another time he had this much fun. He felt as if he could leap from hilltop to hilltop and ski through the valleys. He reached the top of one large hill and stopped to take a rest, even though he was not winded from his physical effort.

As Lance stood on the hilltop he heard a faint whisper of a voice and instinctually knew that was why he was there. He was there to find someone. Somehow he knew he was in this strange place to learn something new about himself or the world. However, he didn't know where to go or how to find the reason he was there. He took a deep breath and slowly exhaled as he closed his eyes. He felt the energy from his body extend out from him like a thousand different arms. In his mind's eye he pictured himself looking like a human octopus with a thousand tentacles. At first the feeling scared him and he instinctively tried to pull back his energy. But his energy tentacles continued to stretch out from his body like feelers to search for the source of the faint whisper he heard. His energy stretched over hills and through valleys and struck something solid that rippled back the message, "Over here!"

For a moment Lance froze and felt the vibration of the words resonate throughout his body. He opened his eyes and half-turned his body in the direction he needed to go, willing himself toward the source. His body glided over the golden grass and he leapt from hilltop to hilltop as the vibrational words "Over here" grew stronger in intensity within his body.

Lance willed himself to move faster, almost flying through the air to move toward the source of the words. As he reached the top of a large hill, he came to an abrupt stop when he saw a stone wall blocking his path at the bottom of the hill. He paused for a moment and stared down at the wall. The stone wall was crude, jagged, and appeared to be hastily built. From what he could see there were no windows or doors, just piled rocks. He wondered why he could not see over the wall if he was technically higher than it as he stood on top of the hill. But he shrugged the thought off and slowly glided down the hill to the base of the wall and gently touched the stones. He felt the energy of the stones pulsate against the palm of his hand.

He looked up and noticed the wall was twice as high as he. He assumed he could climb the wall if he needed to, but in this place he could easily jump to the top. However, at that moment he had no desire to climb or jump to the top; he just wanted to walk or glide alongside of it.

Lance glided the length of the stone wall and dragged the fingers of his left hand against the rough surface, feeling the energy of each stone he touched. He wondered if this was what he was supposed to find. But why? What would finding a stone wall in this mysterious place mean to him? Was this an obstacle? A test? Was the answer on the other side of the wall?

He stopped and turned to face the wall. He wondered if he could conjure up the energy tentacles again. He closed his eyes and slowly exhaled a long deep breath and visualized the energy tentacles extending from his body. He felt his entire body tingle and in his mind's eye could see the energy tentacles waiting to touch the stone wall. He placed both palms of his hands to the wall and the energy tentacles quickly reached out and touched it in a thousand different places. The palms of his hands and the tentacles absorbed the energy from within the stones. At the same time he pushed his energy into the stones and throughout them to find an entrance or a way through the wall. The heat of the passing energy surged through his hands and into his body, causing him to break into a sweat. He continued to focus on searching for a way past the wall. Then unexpectedly he heard a faint whisper of a voice above him, and he slowly lifted his gaze to the top of the wall, spying a man standing on the ridge.

Lance used the energy and leverage of the wall to propel himself upward in a leap and land on the ridge of the wall. But the man he had just seen was gone. How was that possible? The thought quickly dissipated from his mind as he took notice of the beautiful, calm, emerald sea that spread out before him. The white crest of the waves skimmed the surface of the sea and crashed against the base of the stone wall. Silver-metallic dolphins and whales sprang from their watery home into the air and splashed back down into the safety of their domain.

A slight movement caught Lance's attention. He saw the mysterious man waving to him from a stone island surrounded by the sea. Lance leapt from the wall and felt his body float through the air until he reached the island with the man.

The man immediately grabbed Lance's shoulders and hastily spoke. "You must learn how to control your gift."

Confused, Lance questioned him. "What?"

The man squeezed Lance's shoulders tighter and spoke softer but more firmly. "I'm sorry, Lance, for bringing you here so early, but you must understand your gift before it is too late. If we lose you like we have lost the others, then our purpose is lost."

Lance shook himself from the man's grasp. "I don't understand."

"I know, you are young, but you must remember this dream for the rest of your life. If not, all will be lost," explained the man.

"This is a dream?" asked Lance.

"Yes," the man said. "Walk with me and remember what you see."

Lance walked with the man throughout the island and saw people he knew and did not know. Some of them were sitting, standing, or lying on the hard stone. Each person he knew was either laughing or crying. The people he did not know were silent. Lance turned to look at the man walking with him and saw his body shimmer in the purple light like heat waves rising off of hot pavement in the summertime.

Lance slowed to a stop and said, "I don't understand. What does all of this mean?"

The man looked out at the crowd of people they had just walked through. "These are all of the people you have and will come in contact with in your life. The people laughing are ones you have befriended, the people crying are the ones you have wronged, and the people in silence are ones you have not yet met at this time." The man turned and looked out at the emerald sea. "These animals represent the people in the world you have to save with your gift. It is time for you to leave, Lance, but I promise you will see me again."

***

Lance felt an uncontrollable sensation shake his body, and he awoke from his dream with a gasp. He looked around and saw his mother and a stranger in a white coat with a stethoscope around his neck standing in front of him. A rush of terror ran through Lance's body, and he brought both of his knees to his chest. Using his hands, he crawled farther back on the exam table. He tried to remember when he fell asleep, but he couldn't remember falling asleep or why. All he remembered was that it had felt good to close his eyes. He wrapped his arms around his legs and tried to pull them closer to his body for extra comfort. The man in the white coat turned away from Lance, faced his mother, and started talking.

Lance tried to listen and understand the conversation between his mother and the man but they used big words and said things he did not understand. He could tell from the conversation they were talking about him and that something was wrong.

"So it's a sleep disorder?" asked his mother.

"Yes, Mrs. Juddit, it's called narcolepsy. It's a rare sleep disorder that is exhibited by recurrent attacks of sleep. The attacks can vary from a few times to many times throughout a single day and last for a few minutes or hours. When the sleep attack occurs the individual instantaneously falls into REM sleep. The individual can resist the temptation to sleep, but only temporarily. Eventually the individual will fall asleep no matter what the conditions may be. If your son's condition goes untreated, it will be very detrimental for his mental and social well-being."

"If he sleeps more at night will that help him with this condition?"

"Unfortunately not. The total amount of sleep he gets does not reduce the number of attacks he may have in a single day," responded the doctor as he filled out a prescription form.

"What can be done?"

"I am going to prescribe a stimulant that may help. We will start him off with some ephedrine, which has no known side effects. Hopefully this will help reduce his sleep attacks," said the doctor as he handed Mrs. Juddit the slip of paper.

Mrs. Juddit continued, "What about the dreams he tells me about?"

"Sometimes the sleep episodes are accompanied by vivid, frightening dreams. We call them narcoleptic dreams. Hopefully they will subside once we have regulated his medication."

"One more thing, doctor, what about the two moons he says he sees every night?" asked Lance's mother without making eye contact.

"A young boy's vivid imagination," he replied.

Lance's body jerked awake when a stranger sat down in the plastic chair next to him. He focused his eyes on the pharmacist and remembered where he was. Glancing at his watch he swore under his breath when he realized he was late for class.

IV

Cora stood with her feet shoulder-width apart in a strong fighting stance. She faced her opponent, who was taller and stronger. She closed her eyes and let out a long, slow breath to settle her racing mind. With each breath she felt balance and harmony spread from her heart to all points within her body. She momentarily closed her eyes and felt the weight of her small, leather pouch resting against her collarbone. She was ready.

***

Cora stood at the top of the highest foothill in the north. Her long sword stood firm in the ground as her hands lay on the hilt. Although her sword was half her height, in this place her strength could match that of any earthly male. Her long, auburn hair blew behind her as she faced the oncoming wind from the east. Her chiseled arms and legs showed the strength that she could command at any time. From behind, her back flared with a proud V-shape. In the front, her chest was firm and high above her tight abdomen. She was dressed for battle, her sword's sheath hanging from her back, her vest snug for support but revealing enough to distract males of any species. Her legs were covered to mid-thigh with a leather skirt that was snug around her buttocks, but with slits in several places to allow movement. Her boots traveled halfway up her calves with a hidden dagger in the left one. A second dagger was strapped to her right thigh. A small pouch hung from her left hip. Besides her battle scars, the only other mark on her body was a tribal tattoo across her upper back.

Cora felt the rays of the purple sun lick at her bare skin and felt the soft brushes of the golden grass against her legs. She had been to this place many times before and knew to be cautious. The first time she was there was the first time she understood fear. But now she knew why she was there and what she needed to do. She could feel her enemy in the distance and knew it would come to her.

She waited.

***

The Myst, a silver creature known to only a select few, knelt by the emerald stream and cupped a handful of water to drink. It wet its lips with the liquid and let it seep through its three fingers. Down on one knee, it raised its head and saw the back of its enemy at the top of the hill. It had waited many nights to confront her. It felt the rage of hatred boil through its lithe body as the images of its dead family flashed in its mind. Its entire lineage had died at the hand of Cora.

The Myst stood up from the emerald brook. Its fingers grew to sharp points and its teeth grew into sharp fangs. The creature's black-tinted eyes narrowed to slits and its chest heaved up and down in anticipation of the battle. As the creature strode up the hill in long, confident strides to meet its enemy, it fantasized on how it would kill her. It imagined raking its claws across her vulnerable human neck until her head rolled from her shoulders. And then it would howl in victory and delight.

The Myst knew it could change its form and quietly sneak up on its prey in the form of a fog, but it enjoyed stalking her as a predator would its prey. This particular Myst had become obsessed with killing her with its hands. It wanted to drink the life energy that would drain from her body when it ended her existence. The Myst silently twisted and angled its lean body around and past each blade of golden grass without disturbing a single stalk as it ascended the slope toward Cora.

As the Myst approached Cora from behind, it rose to its full height to tower over her by two head lengths. It flexed and extended its clawed hands by its sides and felt the tips of its claws scrape against its outer thighs. Thoughts of ripping Cora's head from her body flashed through its mind. It could hear her screams ripple through its ear holes. It could taste her blood on its two tongues. Its lips parted into a premature devilish grin.

***

Cora felt the presence of the Myst behind her and closed her eyes to steady her breathing. She felt its gentle breath brush against her hair and sensed the hatred of the beast surrounding her like a winter cloak. She steadied the rush of anxiety that surged through her body as the anticipation of the confrontation built inside of her. This was not the first time she had faced one of these creatures. In fact, she had confronted and killed countless of these silver beasts, sometimes more than one at a time, and she always prevailed. She had no reason to think this fight would turn out any differently. The anxiety she felt was not from the inevitable physical confrontation, but the release of the trapped human soul. The consequence of releasing the human soul is what created the anxiety and guilt that she struggled unsuccessfully to hide from her conscious mind.

Unbeknownst to her enemy, Cora tightened and twisted the grip on the hilt of her sword. She felt the Myst's breath quicken against her auburn hair as it prepared to strike at her. The moment came; without warning, Cora spun in an arc toward the creature. Leaving her sword standing in the ground, she extracted a small two-sided dagger from the hilt of the sword. Using the momentum of her spin she ripped a tear through the silver creature's belly with the blade. The tear puked black liquid to the ground. The Myst gripped its stomach and threw its head back in a painful howl. As the scream of pain shattered the silence, Cora struck the creature in the groin with a closed fist, causing the Myst to double over in agony. She grabbed the back of the Myst's head and slammed her knee into its face before shoving it to the ground on its back. Cora straddled the Myst's body and pressed the blood-soaked dagger to its throat. Only then did Cora open her deep purple eyes and stare into the Myst's black, soulless eye holes.

She moved the sharp blade across the throat of the creature and watched its life force escape through the severed wound. As the life force seeped out, it split into two different clouds of mist, one silver and one white. The body of the dead Myst she straddled evaporated to dust and left Cora kneeling on the ground. The silver mist dissipated in the purple light of the sun. The remnants of the white mist wrapped itself around Cora's body like a hug. She closed her eyes and let the remains of the soul thread past through her and into the heavens.

"The soul is free to begin again," she whispered.

V

"Cora!"

"Cora! You won! Back down," commanded her instructor.

Dressed in black stretchy pants and a black uniform, Cora stood over Tom, grasping the rubber knife in her right fist. Tom lay on the mat, bleeding from the nose and trying to catch his breath. Cora took a step back and stood at attention in front of the class. She tried to ignore the stares of shock from the rest of the self-defense class. Tom slowly pushed himself off of the ground in a mixture of disgust and embarrassment.

The instructor briskly walked over to Cora and exclaimed, "Impressive!"

"Thank you," Cora announced, still looking forward.

"Where did you train before here?"

"Nowhere."

The instructor laughed. "Don't play with me, girl."

"Never been formally trained," Cora answered.

The instructor turned his back to Cora to face the class. "Class dismissed!" The class broke up into small cliques, chatting about what they just witnessed. Tom slipped out of the dojo alone and in disgrace. The instructor spun on his heels to face Cora again. "So you have never been trained in the martial arts?"

"That is correct," Cora said in a softer voice.

"Well, I think you're lying to me."

The instructor bent down and picked up Tom's discarded rubber knife and held his hand out for Cora to return hers. She looked down at her hand and realized that her knuckles were still white from gripping the false blade so tightly. She released her grip and handed the prop to her instructor. The instructor shook his head in disbelief, "Knife fighting is an art and you performed it as gracefully as a dance. How in the hell do you explain what you did to Tom?"

Cora locked eyes with the instructor, shrugged slightly, and with a faint smile said, "I have an old soul?"

The instructor chuckled out loud, "An old warrior's soul?" He shook his head and unceremoniously dismissed Cora from the dojo.

The instructor walked off and left Cora alone in the dojo. She turned to face the mirror and did not see a single chalk mark on her from Tom's rubber knife. She grinned to herself in the mirror and her bluish-purple-tinted eyes sparkled back. But the sparkle did not last long because the guilt of what she did to the host body of the Myst struck as a blow to the throat. She collapsed to her knees and covered her face with her hands to try to hide the tears that spilled from her eyes.

VI

On the opposite side of the world, an elderly woman limped past her son's room in the middle of the night. She stopped by his room to peer in to see if he was asleep. With the lights off, she could see the outline of his body under the covers. She quietly left the room with the door slightly open, unaware that the young man's body lay limp under the covers. His heart not beating, his lungs not breathing, and his eyes burnt black.

VII

Dr. James Mac was an older man in his late fifties. In the research facility he always wore an unbuttoned lab coat over his tight-fitting clothes, which were usually a pair of khaki pants, a button-down shirt, and a tie. He was a large man with a very large belly. His belly was so large that the buttons of his shirts strained to stay stitched to the fabric and his belt vanished in the shadows of his overarching stomach. His legs were skinny compared to the rest of his body and he walked with a limp due to a botched surgery on a bunion on his left foot. His personality was equally as large as his frame. He was a generous man with his help, advice, jokes, laughs, and distractibility. He readily admitted to being plagued with attention deficit and hyperactivity disorder and refused to take medication. In the classroom his students would say his favorite saying was, "People, we aren't trying to hit the moon with a rocket from Florida."

But on this day Dr. Mac wore a pair of jeans with a black pullover shirt and a thin jacket. He had traveled to an almost-forgotten cemetery in a small southern Italian town from the west coast of Oregon, which he considered home. He reached into the pouch of a bag he had slung across his shoulder and pulled out rubbing paper and a piece of coal. He pressed the paper over the carved letters on the crypt door and used the coal stick to rub the inscription onto the paper. As he finished the rubbing, two men joined him.

"Is this it, James?" asked the younger of the two men.

Dr. Mac looked over his shoulder and smiled at the young man, "Yes, Mark, I believe it is."

Mark Holland was one of Dr. Mac's hardest-working graduate students. Dr. Mac had more than one graduate student working for him, but Mark had the most potential and determination to carry on Dr. Mac's life's work. What that was exactly Dr. Mac was still trying to figure out for himself. Traditionally trained as a neuropsychiatrist who specialized in sleep disorders, especially narcolepsy, his peers often wondered why he chased down myths and legends about people dream traveling. His research colleagues believed such nonsense was for the mystics and metaphysical community, not for true scientists who used proven scientific methods to support their theories. However, Dr. Mac believed that the hallucinatory dreams that an individual with sleep disorders or narcolepsy experienced was not just his or her imagination, but a form of travel. He believed through a person's dream his or her soul could travel around the world, to new worlds, new dimensions, or even new realities. Privately, he even took the concept a step further. He believed it was possible for a person afflicted with narcolepsy to learn how to control his or her actions and even his or her dreams while asleep.

The only problem was Dr. Mac had not found a way to prove his theory through conventional research. Therefore, he started to look to the past to find clues that could help him prove his theory through sound research. As a child growing up, he was fascinated with archaeology. At one point in time he had actually considered pursuing his PhD in anthropology to become an archaeologist. He chose the mind instead. When he was honest with himself, he enjoyed figuring out how the mind worked in a dysfunctional individual more than he did looking at dusty, long-forgotten objects. What he enjoyed the most was the mystery—asking the question and doing the research to find the answer. So, whether it was a problem with a person's mind or an ancient mystery, Dr. Mac wanted to solve it.

Mark was enthusiastic, energetic, smart, and hard-working. But what Dr. Mac liked most about him was his age and his open mind. Mark was in his early thirties, with prematurely thinning hair and wore wire-rimmed glasses. Dr. Mac thought Mark should take the plunge and shave his head, but Mark seemed to cherish what was left on his cranium. Not that Dr. Mac was a fashion statement himself, but he thought it would make Mark look younger. Mark came to him two years prior, almost begging for the graduate research position. He had reported that he had been working in the consulting industry, but decided to follow his lifelong dream of earning a doctoral degree. Unfortunately, his wife was not as supportive as he had hoped. She gave him an ultimatum. He took a different route. They divorced, he quit his job, and now he was a poor PhD student. The pay as a research assistant was minimal, but he supplemented his income working as a tutor and at the used bookstore in town. Mark had only one more year until he completed his dissertation and then Dr. Mac would have to find a new student to groom. He hoped that Mark would stay at the university and continue working with him, but he had lost too many other students to the same promise over the years to even get his hopes up about Mark.

Mark stepped closer, "What does it say?" he asked.

Before Dr. Mac could answer, a nervous old caretaker recited the inscription from memory. "Gavin Arbitor, born 1085, died 1110. May he sleep less in death then he did in life. May his dreams become his reality."

Dr. Mac surmised that the old caretaker was in his late seventies, but he could be older or younger. He assumed burying people for a living either aged you beyond your years or simply would not let you be buried yourself. The old man had a permanent hunch in his upper back that forced him to watch his feet while he walked—which was probably a good thing because the old man's right foot turned inward and his left foot turned outward, which caused his gait to be slow and shuffled. When he did straighten up to speak, Dr. Mac could see the pain the man suffered as he hissed the words through his missing teeth. Dr. Mac deduced the man's hunch was from all of the years of shoveling graves, but it could have been a genetic trait passed down through the generations. He thought for a moment to ask if he learned his trade from his father, but he thought it better to not ask—not because he was afraid of upsetting the man, but more because he assumed that the caretaker that sealed Gavin Arbitor in his tomb in 1110 was probably this old man's twentieth great-grandfather, or something to that effect. Instead of inquiring of the old man's genealogical history, he simply inclined his head in agreement and said, "Very good, sir. May I ask why you know this inscription by heart?"

The old caretaker chuckled a throaty laugh and shook his head in disbelief—not disbelief at or in Dr. Mac, but disbelief to the unfathomable mysteries of the dead. In broken English, the old man replied, "'Cause I have been to this tomb many times before," as he pushed past Dr. Mac and Mark to reach the lock of the crypt door.

Mark gave Dr. Mac a quizzical look and asked, "Why?"

The old man spun on his heels faster than Dr. Mac or Mark thought could be possible for a person trapped in such a misshapen body. The caretaker tried to straighten his body as tall as it would go in order to shove his finger in the professor's face. "I told you on the phone, Gavin Arbitor is not dead!" hissed the old man in broken English through painfully gritted teeth. Hunching over, he dropped to his heels and mumbled almost inaudibly, "I've heard him, begging to be released."

Mark shot Dr. Mac a look and the professor chose to ignore the comment, instead rolling up the rubbing paper to place in his shoulder bag. "Please, sir, just open the door," commanded Dr. Mac as he took two steps back to give the old caretaker room to maneuver. He purposefully refused to look at Mark, knowing exactly what he was thinking, because he was thinking the same thing.

The old man must be delusional, thought Dr. Mac. There is no way that Gavin Arbitor is over nine hundred years old. Even if he could live that long, what would he eat in a sealed crypt? No, it was not humanly possible for anyone to live over nine hundred years. The last written account of a human living to be over nine hundred years is in the Bible, and many scholars debate if that is even real. What would the caretaker gain by telling him false ghost stories? Unless, thought Dr. Mac, the old man was trying to prevent anyone from entering the crypt because he was hiding something. That didn't make sense either, because the old man knew for over three months that he was coming to exhume the body. That would have given the caretaker more than enough time to remove any hidden treasures he stored in this forgotten tomb.

The caretaker turned back to the crypt door and tugged a ring of keys from his coat pocket. He took a few minutes to fumble with it before finding a distinct piece of metal that did not resemble a key. The old man pushed it into the lock and turned. All of the men heard the loud click as the locking mechanism released. The old man removed the key and turned to look at Mark, "You're younger than

I," spat out the man in his broken English as he gestured toward the door.

Mark glanced at the doctor in confirmation, and Dr. Mac inclined his head to give his permission. Mark restrained himself from exhaling out loud in protest and gripped the handle to the crypt door. He tugged, but it did not move. The caretaker smiled, but only his feet witnessed the action. Mark tugged again with no success. This time the caretaker chuckled audibly out loud and patted Mark on the back.

"Move away, boy. In my old age I forget that young men no longer have true strength," said the old man as he shouldered Mark out of the way.

Mark conceded to the man and was anxious to watch the older gentleman fail at opening the crypt door. The old man grunted once and pulled open the door. A rush of stale air and dust assaulted the three men standing in the morning sunlight. The caretaker brushed the stench of the air away and hid the grin that stretched across his lips, knowing that the younger man was beside himself in disgust. Dr. Mac thought he heard a low growl emanate from Mark's throat, but that would be ridiculous. However, Mark did growl and was surprised at his own hostility toward the old man.

The caretaker ran his bony fingers through his thick, white, stringy hair and peered into the open crypt. Absentmindedly he drew the sign of the cross over his chest and muttered under his breath, "Forgive us, Lord, for disturbing a tomb that was never meant to be opened." He turned and faced Dr. Mac. The old man gritted through the pain and straightened himself to his full height to lock eyes with the professor. "This is on you and that boy," he hissed at him through his teeth as he blindly pointed at Mark. "You have forced me to disturb the slumber of the demon. You have forced me to disturb the ghosts that haunt this tomb."

Dr. Mac wanted to tell the old man he was being ridiculous. He wanted to tell the man that demons and ghosts did not exist. But there was something in the man's eyes that made him stop and pause for a moment. The caretaker believed what he said. He believed that this tomb embodied all of the ghost stories originating from spooky graveyards. So he was unable to reassure the old man that no harm would befall him. That ghosts, or spirits, or demons would never haunt him. But he could not bring himself to say those words. Instead he reached out and touched the man's shoulder, "You are right my friend, this falls on me." He paused and looked at Mark, "But only me."

The three men stood in silence for a moment, staring into the open tomb.

The old man broke the silence first, "Well, Doc, since you are taking the blame for this disturbance, you first."

Dr. Mac shot the man a surprised look and Mark tried to restrain his laugh. The caretaker patted Dr. Mac on his back, "No worries, I'll pray for you."

Mark laughed, "Yeah, me too, James," he said as he followed the doctor into the tomb with the old caretaker on his heels.

"Thanks," Dr. Mac muttered as the darkness consumed him.

VIII

Dr. Mac brushed the old cobwebs away as he and Mark walked into the dark entrance to the crypt. Once inside, Mark and Dr. Mac turned on their flashlights and traced the beams of light around the small stone room. Columns stood in each of the four corners and the stone ceiling was carved with interlocking concentric circles. On the east and west walls were two faded murals made from colored marble. The north wall contained a trellis over a second door with dead vines camouflaging most of the area. The tile on the floor had similar concentric circles as the ceiling.

The doctor wandered over to the east wall while Mark stood in the middle of the room.

"How is this a crypt if there is no church?" asked Mark.

The old man spoke from one of the dark corners, "The Germanic tribes destroyed the church centuries ago. This structure was built to protect the entrance to the crypt."

Mark asked, "Who built the structure?"

The old caretaker shrugged his shoulders, "From what I was told, a group called the Seekers of the Liberators."

Mark flashed the beam of light in the man's direction and watched him move toward the trellis, breaking away the dead vines to reach the second door. He was going to join the man, but Dr. Mac called him over.

"Mark, what do you make of this?"

Mark joined the professor and added his light to the mural. They both saw a landscape with fields of tall golden grass leading to a cliff's edge. The cliff's edge was impossibly high and merged with a crashing emerald ocean. In the fields of golden grass it looked as if hundreds of silver humanoid creatures were gathered near the cliff's edge. From the sky it appeared that several silver beams of light were descending to the cliffs. Dr. Mac reached up and brushed the dust and dirt from the tile representing the sky.

"Purple," he whispered.

Mark echoed him, "Purple? A purple sky?"

Dr. Mac used the palm of his hand to brush away more of the tile representing the sky and nodded his head in agreement, "Yes, I think it is."

Mark shrugged and walked off to explore another part of the chamber.

Dr. Mac traced his finger down from the purple sky to one of the silver humanoid creatures. He whispered "Lance," but before he could continue his thought, Mark called him over to the center of the room.

Mark stood in the middle of the room tracing his flashlight beam toward the ceiling. "It's a labyrinth," he announced.

Dr. Mac looked up and nodded his head in agreement. "Yes, it is."

"Interesting that a labyrinth design would be etched in the ceiling of a Christian-based crypt," said Mark.

Dr. Mac shined his light toward the floor, "Two actually. I'm sure the lines on the floor mimic what is on the ceiling. However, I am not surprised. Labyrinths are symbolic representations of the universe and the power within a human soul."

"True, but in Christian religions isn't God the universe and power within?" asked Mark.

"Yes, I am sure in some circles that could be argued. But in non-Christian-based religions or philosophies of thought, an adept can use a labyrinth to transform himself," replied Dr. Mac.

"How?"

"Usually through meditation," answered Dr. Mac as he squatted to trace the lines of the labyrinth on the floor.

"But transform himself into what?"

Dr. Mac stood back up, "Not a what, but a state of being. A state of unity with the universe, connection to the power within, or to God." He walked off to the west wall satisfied that he had given Mark enough information to process.

The west wall contained a similar mural with a purple sky and an emerald waterfall cascading into an isolated pond. But instead of silver humanoid creatures, there were two naked humans, a man and a woman. The man stood in the water up to his waist while the woman floated on her back with her eyes closed. His hands supported her upper back while her crimson-colored hair floated in the water over his arms.

Dr. Mac was unable to fully examine the west wall mural because the caretaker had opened the second door and beckoned them to join him.

The three men descended a flight of stone steps into a darkness that was hardly penetrated by the two flashlights. At the bottom of the stone steps the caretaker struck a match and held it to a torch hanging on the wall to his right. He took the lighted torch and moved around the room, igniting five other torches before replacing the first one to its holder. The Doctor and Mark turned off their flashlights and through the flickering firelight saw a stone casket on a pedestal in the middle of the chamber.

Dr. Mac and Mark slowly approached the casket and quickly noticed that the lid to the casket was skewed. Dr. Mac peered into the casket while Mark aimed the flashlight beam in the coffin to illuminate the body within.

"I presume that is Gavin Arbitor," stated Mark in a hushed whisper.

Dr. Mac nodded his head in acknowledgment.

Mark turned toward the caretaker and asked, "Why is the lid like this?"

The caretaker pushed off of the wall he was leaning against by the stairs and made a motion to look as if it was the first time he ever saw it. He shrugged his shoulders, "Grave robbers, I assume."

"How is that possible? The tomb was sealed," countered Mark.

Dr. Mac leaned into the coffin to peer more closely at the body.

The caretaker got testy and snapped at Mark. "Boy, you are lucky this tomb is even here! It is close to a thousand years old."

Mark sighed audibly and started searching the rest of the tomb. The caretaker plopped on the bottom step of the stairs and mumbled under his breath, "I can feel the evilness seeping into my very bones."

Dr. Mac glanced at the caretaker for a moment and then went back to examining the body. "Sir, do you know if this body was embalmed?" asked Dr. Mac.

"How old do I look to you?" snapped the caretaker.

The doctor smiled at the man's feistiness and fear. "Just asking. Even though the casket was open, it appears as if the body never deteriorated, which is simply amazing. Perhaps it is the climate that preserved the body."

Curiosity got the better of the caretaker and he moved from his seated position to stand by the doctor's side and peered into the casket. "It's because the man never died," whispered the caretaker.

Dr. Mac looked at the caretaker. "How is that possible? Gavin Arbitor would be over nine hundred years old if that were the case."

The caretaker shrugged his shoulders and moved off to the stairs to sit again. "Ask the Yogi Masters who prolong death and can manifest themselves in two places at once."

The comment took Dr. Mac by surprise. He smiled and asked, "Who are you?"

"Pft, I'm the caretaker of this cemetery and nothing more." But he turned and straightened as tall as his back would allow and said, "I have worked in this cemetery for almost sixty years and I tell you, many nights I have heard someone trying to get out of this tomb. Day or night, while I walked my rounds I would hear his cries and moans as I passed this crypt. When I was a child my father would ignore the sounds and dismiss them as my overactive imagination. When my father died and I took over this hellhole, I opened the outer door to this crypt the first night and I waited." The caretaker paused to catch his breath.

"And then I heard him," said the old man as he shook his head at the memory. "I heard his pleas to be released just on the other side of the second door." The caretaker sat on the steps and whispered, "I almost had the strength to open the second door, but my courage slipped away from me like an owl in the night, and I ran."

The man sat silent for a time and then finished. "You can tell me that I am crazy, but I know what I heard that night and every time before and after that."

Dr. Mac had no response to the old man's story and an awkward silence fell within the room. The caretaker chuckled softly and slapped his knees to stand up. "I'll get my sons to transfer the body to the travel casket and load it into your vehicle," announced the caretaker.

Dr. Mac nodded his head in acknowledgment and watched the old man disappear into the darkness of the stairs. He glanced at Mark, who looked apprehensive, and then moved off to explore the rest of the crypt. With the body of Gavin Arbitor being transferred to his research facility in Oregon, he knew he would have more time to examine it and the contents of the coffin at his leisure. However this would be the one and only time he would have access to the crypt. Therefore, he needed to make the best of his time.

As the caretaker's four sons worked on preparing the body to be moved, Dr. Mac walked around the crypt and traced his fingers against the walls. He walked at a slow pace with his eyes half-closed so he could feel every bump and dip in the stone walls. He traced his fingers high and low and at times used both palms of his hands to feel the surface. On the west wall Dr. Mac paused for a moment, feeling many small grooves in the wall. He pulled out his rubbing paper and pressed it over the grooves, rubbing vigorously. He watched as a string of Latin words appeared on the paper. He pulled the paper from the wall and realized the passage was from a greater body of text.

"Mark, I think I found something," called Dr. Mac.

When Mark reached his side he continued. "Feel the wall," commanded Dr. Mac. As Mark did so he continued, "I believe this wall contains a story of some sort."

Mark nodded his head in acknowledgment. "The entire wall is covered with words."

The two men smiled at each other and they systematically started to transfer the Latin text on the west wall to the rubbing papers. The process took several hours to complete, and the caretaker sat on the bottom step of the stairs muttering under his breath the entire time. Once in a while Dr. Mac would notice the old man sipping whisky from a metal flask and then hiding the evidence under his coat.

When the two men completed the task, Mark gently shook the caretaker's shoulder to wake him from his drunken stupor. The old man awoke with a scream and kicked at Mark, thinking he was a ghost. His whisky spilled when he kicked and he cursed under his breath for being so careless. Mark reached down to offer the man a hand to get up. The caretaker swatted his hand away and unsteadily rose to his feet. The three men ascended the stairs and Mark assisted the caretaker in closing both crypt doors.

As Dr. Mac and Mark drove away, the caretaker spat on the ground after them and walked off into the fading sunlight.

IX

The smell of stale death struck Lance as he walked into the sterile, red-brick building. He wondered if anyone else ever smelled the same stench he did? As he looked around the lobby it was clear that everyone there was either ignoring the smell or was used to the foul odor. He walked up to the receptionist's desk and waited for the elderly woman to acknowledge his presence. When she looked up at him he smiled and said, "I'm here to see my father, Mr. Juddit."

The woman flipped through a pack of wrinkled papers that were stained with coffee rings. Her equally wrinkled finger with the gaudy nail polish slid down each page until the woman found his dad's name. She looked up at him, "And you are?" she asked.

"His son, Lance," he said with a smile, but then mumbled, "the same guy that comes every week."

The older woman glanced at the paper and then back at him, "Excuse me? Did you say something?"

Lance shook his head no.

The older woman handed Lance a piece of paper and asked him to sign his name and note the time he had arrived. As Lance signed the paper he quickly scanned to see if anyone else had been to visit his dad. Nope. Just him. He handed the paper back to the receptionist and turned to walk off. She called after him, "Room L411." Lance looked over his shoulder and smiled. He knew.

He walked down three hallways and climbed four flights of stairs to reach his dad's room. He quietly pushed open the door and watched his dad for a few moments. His dad stood by the sink drying a coffee cup with a paper towel, meticulously cleaning and drying every surface of the mug. Lance smiled at the memory of his dad teaching him how to do the dishes. It was not just about washing the dishes, but also cleaning the counters, the table, and sweeping the floor. It was about taking pride in the chore and doing it right. Pride. Pride in yourself. Pride in your accomplishment, no matter what it was. He learned that from his dad.

"Can I help you?" asked Lance's dad, which broke Lance from his thoughts.

"Hi, Dad," said Lance. "It's me, your son."

Lance's dad stopped drying the coffee mug and looked at him with a perplexed expression. "My son is dead," said the man simply and placed the mug in the cupboard above the sink before hanging the paper towel on the drying rack.

Lance closed his eyes and breathed through the tears that wanted to fall from his eyes. With his eyes still closed he whispered, "He's not dead." Lance paused and whispered to himself, "He was just asleep."

The man looked at Lance and picked up the paper towel he had just laid down and a plate from the drying rack. He showed Lance the plate and started to dry it, "The military taught me how to wash dishes." He looked at the plate and smiled. "And how to dry them."

Lance moved into the efficiency that his dad was now forced to live in so he could get around-the-clock care. He sat in the chair his father kept by the door and took his shoes off. This was usually as far as he ever got into his dad's room. "I'm a damn good dishwasher," said his dad as he put the plate away.

"You're also a damn good dad," said Lance.

"What?" asked Lance's dad. "I didn't hear you."

"They also taught you how to be a marksman and a computer programmer," said Lance.

His dad looked at him and shrugged his shoulders, "I don't know about all that, but washing dishes, that is something special." He paused. "And peeling potatoes," he said with a smile of satisfaction.

"You never peeled potatoes for Mom," stated Lance. He was not sure why he said it. Maybe out of anger. Maybe frustration. Maybe spite. But he regretted saying it as soon as the words passed his lips. He was better than that. He had more patience than that. Well, he thought he did.

Lance looked up at his dad, who was staring at him. Lance held his gaze and his father said, "Your mother was a great woman."

Lance blinked. He remembered. His dad remembered. He smiled and confirmed, "Yes, she is."

Lance's father looked at him, "Is?" He shook his head. "No, she is dead. Just like my son." And went back to drying a fork he must have used for dinner.

Lance sighed out loud. "I'm taking real classes this time, Dad." He paused. "You might ask why." He hung his head and mumbled, "It would be nice if you asked why." He looked up at his dad. His dad continued to dry the fork. "I'm tired of being alone. I want some company. I want more than just cyber-friends," said Lance. He felt pathetic saying the words out loud. But they needed to be said. "I have new medication to keep me awake. I think I have a good chance of doing well. You always thought I was gifted and so smart," Lance said hopefully. "Maybe you could come to my graduation when I finish?" asked Lance as he watched his dad pick up a spoon to dry. The spoon he probably used to stir the sugar in his coffee.

Lance's father stopped and stared past Lance. "My son, I miss him."

Lance slowly stood and whispered, "I'm right here, Dad."

His dad moved closer to Lance. He reached out his hand toward Lance's face, "My son was so handsome and so smart. He had a gift. He could visit different worlds. He saw things I only dreamed of while I slept." His eyes focused on Lance and he pulled his hand away. "Who are you?"

Lance wanted to scream. He wanted to scream in his father's face to jog his memory that his only son was alive. He wanted to scream at the universe for ruining his father's life by stealing his memory. He wanted his confidant. He wanted his best friend. He wanted the one person in the entire world who never doubted him. He wanted the one person that always believed him. He wanted his dad back.

Instead, he leaned in close to his dad's ear and whispered, "I'm an angel and I am here to tell you that your son loves you and can't wait to see you again." He stepped back into the doorway and started to pull the door shut. Before the door closed his father grabbed it and stopped it. He smiled and said, "Tell him I'm proud to be his father."

Lance pulled the door closed before the tears could spill from his eyes. He turned and leaned his back against the door and patted his chest twice—the sign language that he and his dad shared while he was growing-up. Two pats to the chest meant "I love you." It was their secret.

He slowly breathed out to gather his strength and walked away. Before he reached the entrance of the building his cell phone vibrated. He pulled it out of his back pocket and saw that it was a text message from his mother. She was asking how his father was. He texted back the word "Fine" and sent it. He was not angry with his mom. He knew Dad's dementia was hardest on her. Still, sometimes she just texted at the wrong time.

X

Cora pulled off her shirt as she walked into the bathroom and gently kicked the door closed with her heel. She glanced at herself in the mirror and grabbed the towel that hung from the back of the door. She reached into the bathtub to feel the temperature of the water and turned the handles to the cold and hot water to off. She hung her towel on a hook next to the tub and used both hands to slide her panties off to the ground. Lastly, before stepping into the warm water, she pulled off the small leather pouch that hung around her neck and placed it on the bathmat next to the bathtub.

Cora slid her nude body into the water and closed her eyes to welcome the embrace of the water and bubbles. She submerged her head to wet her hair and then pushed back up from the surface of the water and ran her hands and fingernails over her face to push her tangle of hair back over her scalp. Blindly reaching over the side of the tub, Cora felt for the leather pouch and picked it up. Relaxing her head on the cold porcelain of the bathtub, she held it in front of her. She swung the pouch in front of her as if she was trying to hypnotize herself. Sometimes it worked, but this evening she was missing her mom, which always made it hard for her to relax. She wished she had more from her mother than just a small leather pouch. Be it that the contents of the leather pouch, according to her mother, were the most important gift she could ever give her daughter.

Cora stared past the swinging pouch and remembered the day her mother gave it to her. Their neighbors always teased that Cora's mother was a witch or a medicine woman of some sort because she was always rummaging through the forest for various herbs, flowers, and weeds. Plus it never helped that her mother had visitors late into the night. If Cora had pressed the neighbors, she was sure they would have also said her mom was a lady of the night, to put it nicely, but Cora knew the truth. Her mother was part of some group called the Seekers of the Liberators. Truthfully, as a young girl, Cora never understood what that meant. To her, all the visitors were friends and family. She often wondered about her father, but Cora's mom always avoided that subject.

One night, when Cora was a teenager her mother took her hand and led her out into the forest. Together, they tracked a black cat that lived on the edge of the forest. Well, maybe not tracked, corrected Cora; the cat willingly went to her mother. As her mother sat cross-legged in the grass stroking the fur of the cat, she abruptly snapped its neck. Cora gasped, but contained her words when her mother simply stood up and walked into the woods. Cora obediently followed. They walked for a great distance through the dark night until they came to a clearing in the trees. Cora remembered the moon was high and full overhead. There was no need for a flashlight because the clearing was almost as bright as during the day. Her mother sat by a ring of stones and made a fire. Cora sat next to her and watched.

Her mother pulled out a long knife and cut the head of the black cat off. She then cut off the tail, tossing the body into the flames of the fire. Her mother mumbled something under her breath as the flames of the fire licked at the body of the cat. Cora thought her mother said thank you in her mumbles, but was never sure. She remembered the smell of burning flesh and fur more than the words. Her mother skinned the skull and tail of the cat and tossed the disregarded remains into the fire, except for the eyes and tongue. Those she placed into a pouch by her side. Using a large pestle she ground the skull and tail bones into a fine dust. Reaching back into the pouch by her side she sprinkled some herbs into the bone dust. Then she finally squeezed liquid from each cat eye into the mortar. The cat's tongue she decided to keep for another time. Mixing the contents into a paste, she poured everything into a leather pouch and sealed it shut.

Cora's mother kneeled in front of Cora. She motioned for Cora to incline her head forward. As she did, her mother placed the leather pouch around her neck. A part of Cora wanted to stop her out of disgust. But she did not; instead she looked into her mother's eyes.

Her mom clasped both of her hands, briefly smiled, and softly spoke as if she did not want to disturb the stillness of the night. "You are of my blood." She reached up to stroke her daughter's face. "You have a gift that the Seekers will call upon in time. You are greater than all of us."

Her mother smiled and looked down at both of Cora's hands. "I know you think I'm crazy with all of my superstitions, but I know things of this world that have remained hidden for hundreds of years." She paused and looked up at the night sky. "But now it is time for you to know and be prepared."

Her mother reached down and lifted the pouch that hung just at Cora's collarbone. "This will guide you to a place—" she paused again almost as if she was trying not to cry "—a place to liberate us all from secrets that are forced upon us." Her mother stood and looked down at her daughter with a sadness in her eyes that Cora had never forgotten. She leaned down and kissed her daughter's forehead and moved to whisper into Cora's ear. "You can come home when you see the portal in the flames and the two moons in the sky above." Then her mother moved off into the dark forest alone.

Cora sat for a long time alone by the fire contemplating what her mother had said. She remembered staring into the fire for so long that images of silver humans danced in the flames and purple-tinted flames burst from the embers. Then she heard the scream. A scream she would never forget nor hear again. A scream that broke her from the trance of the fire. She leapt to her feet and dashed toward the tree-line back to her house. Before crashing into the branches of the forest she momentarily glanced up to the night sky and thought she saw two moons high overhead. When she reached her house it was engulfed in flames and her mother was gone. She lost everything that night, except for the pouch that hung around her neck. Cora squeezed the pouch trying to remember her mother's face, but the image was out of her grasp.

Cora exhaled and felt the cooling temperatures of the water around her body as it rippled from her slight movements. She used her foot to reach up and turn on the hot water. She let the bathtub fill and shut it off again. Clutching the pouch in her hands, she rested them on her stomach and slowed her breathing to a rhythmic pace, drifting deeper into a meditative state with each inhale and exhale.

***

Cora drifted through the clouds of the purple sky and smiled as she felt the cool air brush against her bare skin. She twisted and twirled in the evening sky as if she were swimming in a pool of water. She felt safe and secure as she glided over the golden stalks of grass and skimmed the surface of the foothills that rippled the ground beneath her. In the distance she could see the Cliffs of Eternity separating the Northern and Southern Hemispheres. Off to the East she could see the Oasis of Calm and to the West was the Castle.

Cora had never ventured to the West or to what she called the Castle. She spied the structure only from afar and from the cover of clouds. She was not completely sure the structure was a castle, or even man-made. From the distance it appeared to be a medieval castle. However, it could have been rock formations in the likeness of a castle. She paused in her flight and hung motionless in the sky, wondering why she had never gone to explore the structure. There was no reason why she had not. She just never had an overwhelming urge to explore it further. Even now, she had no urge to satisfy her curiosity.

Cora turned her attention to the Cliffs of Eternity and quickly forgot about the Castle as she flew toward the crashing waves of the Emerald Ocean. As she glided closer to the cliffs she saw a humanoid figure walking. Her purple-tinted eyes focused on the humanoid creature and realized it was a man. His dark hair was cut short and his back was strong and tapered from his shoulders to his waist. Cora floated down behind him and hung in the air just within arm's reach.

Her body tingled in anticipation and nervously reached out to touch the stranger on the shoulder. At the same time the man turned to face her. As his face came into view he faded away before her eyes.

Cora let her hands linger in the empty air. She rubbed her fingers together and could feel the energy residue that the man left behind. She felt his energy pulsate and merge with her own. It was strong. Stronger than any energy she had felt before, except for maybe her mother's. It warmed her and strengthened her in a way that she had not felt since her mother's touch. She opened her eyes, hoping to see him or maybe even her mother. But she was alone on the cliff's edge. She exhaled audibly in frustration and stared down at the waves crashing against the massive boulders below. A thin smile stretched across her lips when she realized that she wanted to feel his energy again.

She needed to feel it again.

***

Cora opened her eyes after the twelfth breath and felt her lips stretch into a smile.

"Who is he?" she wondered out loud.

XI

As he slept in class, Lance's eyes danced under his closed lids as his head rested against the back of the auditorium chair. A soft hand shook his shoulder, gently at first, then more forcefully to wake him. Lance's eyes snapped open to the gaze of an angry instructor. He cleared his throat and pushed himself up to a seated position. He felt the hand that woke him slide off of his shoulder. The instructor frowned and turned away to continue his current boring lecture on the union wars of the 1950s in the hills of West Virginia. Lance rubbed the sleep from his eyes with the heels of his hands. He turned to face the classmate who sat directly behind him every day, woke him up every day, but never spoke. The young woman held his gaze for a quick second. Then she quickly turned back to watch the instructor gesture wildly with enthusiasm about the coal miners who lived and worked in West Virginia. Lance wrote "Thank you" on a sheet of paper and reached back to place the note on the keyboard of the girl's laptop computer. She did not look at the note right away. When the instructor turned his back on the class she handed him the paper back and had written, "Sophia."

Lance fought to stay awake the rest of the class but was unsuccessful in his attempts and squeezed in two more naps before the end of the class. He found American History fascinating, but the instructor was a bore. Narcolepsy or not, thought Lance, this pathetic professor could solve anyone's insomnia. Lance had known the risk of signing up for a lecture class would mean he would likely sleep the semester away. He had hoped with his new medication he would be able to handle the situation. Three weeks into the semester and he had stayed awake the equivalent of one ninety-minute class. The next twelve weeks were going to be painful. However, on the bright side, he had finally gotten the girl's name, so there was no way he was going to drop the class now. He would just have to find a way to stay awake for the hour and a half each week.

Lance stood just under six feet tall and had short black hair. His body was chiseled and cut from the many outdoor activities he participated in, not from the time he spent in the gym. He was older than most of the college students in his classes, not because he was slow, but because of his medical condition. When class ended, Lance followed Sophia out into the hallway. Her tight blue jeans drew attention to her slim figure. Inevitably, he got caught looking at her backside when she turned around to confront him. Embarrassed, he cleared his throat. "I'm Lance." He stuck his hand out to shake hers.

Sophia's red lips stretched into a smile and she shook his hand. Lance thought he saw her eyes sparkle when they shook hands, but he could have imagined that in his hope that she was attracted to him. She moved a strand of hair from her face when she let go of his hand.

"You know, Lance, that is the first time you thanked me for waking you up in class," stated Sophia.

"Really? I've fallen asleep in that class before?" asked Lance jokingly.

Sophia snickered. "Every class, just like in your statistics class," said Sophia as she turned to walk down the hall.

Lance thought for a minute. "Hey, how do you know I fall asleep in stats?" he asked as he chased after her.

Stopping at the door before she pushed it open to walk out in the sunlight, Sophia half-turned to face him. "I sit behind you, two rows back."

Holding the door open for Sophia, he said, "No wonder it always feels like I am being watched," Lance smiled.

Sophia blushed as she walked out into the campus commons. Lance followed her out and walked alongside her.

Sophia looked at Lance and asked, "Why do you fall asleep all the time?"

Lance smirked. "Direct, aren't you?"

Sophia smiled and asked, "Is that a problem?"

"No," replied Lance a bit more quickly than he expected.

"So why are you always sleeping?" persisted Sophia.

"Well if you had more time than just a walk between classes, I would be more than happy to tell you my tragic story," smiled Lance.

"How about over coffee at the pub?" asked Sophia.

"Now?"

"Yes, silly," said Sophia as she slid her arm around Lance's and led him to the pub down the block.

XII

"It's called narcolepsy. It's a sleep disorder," Lance said as he placed his coffee cup back on the table. Sophia sat across from him, enjoying her hot cup of coffee.

"I guess it would be hard for you to understand what I go through every day," continued Lance as Sophia listened. "According to studies, one in every two thousand people have narcolepsy. However, most people go undiagnosed or misdiagnosed for years, plus everyone's condition varies," he said as he sipped his coffee.

Lance continued. "Narcolepsy is classified in the medical field as a neurological disorder. To put it simply, someone with narcolepsy falls into REM sleep almost immediately. I could sleep for a few minutes or a few hours several times a day. This sets a very thin framework for a successful social life," said Lance as he paused to look into his coffee. Sophia reached across the small round table and squeezed his hand, letting the touch linger.

Lance looked up at Sophia and continued, "Usually people with this condition have poor grades in school, inability to concentrate or memorize, loss of several jobs throughout their life, and low self-esteem. It's understandable we have the tendency to become alcoholics, depressed, have high divorce rates, and no sex life," smiled Lance, hoping the last comment would get some reaction out of Sophia. But her eyes did not even flinch. I hope this isn't a lost cause, he thought.

"I was diagnosed when I was a kid, by a scientist out in Oregon. The funny thing is, he believes the best way to cure anything is to understand the past." Lance paused to take a drink. "'If you understand the past, then you can cure the future,' were his words exactly. Well, he hasn't found a cure yet," said Lance.

"Does he still treat you?" asked Sophia.

"Yes and no. I get my medication from another doctor, but I keep in contact with Dr. Mac, just in case he finds something," said Lance.

Still holding his hand, she said, "It looked like you were dreaming today in class. Does that always happen?"

"Hallucinations. The person having the dream thinks they are real and sometimes cannot tell the difference from the dream or reality. The hallucinations usually only last a few seconds and occur when you are waking up or falling asleep." Lance pulled an orange bottle of medication from his backpack, "That is why I will take stimulants and antidepressants the rest of my life, to try to be normal."

Sophia sat up and leaned across the table and kissed Lance on the cheek. "You seem normal enough to me. And besides, what is normal anyway?"

Lance placed his hand over his mouth to conceal his yawn.

Sophia smiled. "Are you close to graduating?"

Lance nodded his head. "Yes. I have one more semester after this. How about you?"

Sophia leaned back in her chair and took a drink of her coffee. "One more year after this." Her cell phone buzzed and she picked it up to glance at it. She frowned and said to Lance, "I have to run to a meeting with a professor. I hope you don't mind."

Lance smiled, but he did mind. He was enjoying himself. He liked her company. He shook his head no. "I don't mind. I understand."

Sophia reached over. "Let me see your phone so I can give you my number."

Lance obediently handed his cell phone to her. He watched as she typed in her name and number. She handed it back to him with a smile. "I had fun. Thank you," she said as she stood. Before she turned and walked off she encouraged, "Text me soon."

Lance smiled and said, "I will." He watched her walk out of the coffee shop and wondered if it was too soon to text her.

XIII

Lance rolled out of bed onto the floor to perform a set of fifty push-ups. After finishing he pressed himself off the beige carpeted floor and walked over to the full-length mirror hanging on the door. He frowned at the nighttime reflection of the two moons in the mirror from the open window behind him. It was still nighttime, not that he was surprised. Glancing at the clock, the red neon numbers read 3:15 a.m. Feeling his stomach growl, he made his way to the kitchen in search of food. He did not bother pulling pants or shorts over his briefs when he woke up in the middle of the night and wandered through his apartment, because he lived alone. He preferred to live alone. He preferred to walk around half-naked, fully-naked too. He enjoyed the freedom. As he passed the computer desk in the living room on his way to the kitchen, he reached under the desk and pressed the power button. As the computer hummed to life, he walked to the kitchen and grabbed a breakfast bar and a prepackaged bottle of orange juice from the refrigerator.

The light from the computer screen illuminated the small living area and Lance did not bother to turn on any other lights. He often wondered what people thought when they drove past his apartment and saw lights on in his apartment at all different hours. Most likely they thought he was a pervert surfing inappropriate websites and chat rooms at ungodly hours in the night. Or maybe they thought he was working on a novel in hopes of being a published writer. He smiled and shook his head; he doubted that. Before he ate the breakfast bar he pulled on a shirt. He had no problem walking around naked, but he never ate naked or without a shirt on. His parents had taught him at an early age it was respectful to always wear a shirt when eating. They never said anything about pants. He sat at the desk and scrolled through several e-mail messages and deleted half of them because of their uselessness to his life. Then one message caught his attention: a message from Sophia.

Hi Lance,

Sorry to bug, just wanted to say hi. I haven't seen you in class and was worried about you. Hope you aren't sleeping on me! Lol :):}

MU <3 Sophia

Lance clicked on the reply message button with the mouse.

Hi S, You could never bug me, feel free to bug anytime. Been sleeping and doing homework that is long overdue. I'm sure I didn't miss anything in class except for you :} Maybe we can grab a bite to eat soon?

L

Lance clicked the send button with the mouse and minimized the e-mail screen, not expecting a reply from her for at least five more hours. He figured since he was awake he should at least attempt to finish proofreading the last short story he wrote. As the file loaded, he opened the bottle of orange juice and took a long drink. Scrunching his face in a look of disgust, he quickly remembered that orange juice and the chocolate of the breakfast bar didn't mix well. One of these days he would remember that it was a bad combination.

Once the file was loaded, he yawned and picked up a marked-up draft of his story and made corrections to the electronic version on the computer. Happy with the changes he made, he printed a clean copy of the final version. As he waited for the pages on the printer he sucked on a piece of hard candy. When the print job was done he grabbed the pages from the printer and sat back in his chair to read the story again for the four hundredth time.

XIV

A strong wind blew against Lance's face as he stood in the golden field of grass. In the distance he could see dozens of rolling, golden hills surrounding each side of him. The purple sky and silver clouds were foreign to his eyes, but at the same time familiar and beautiful. He walked through the field and brushed his hands against the tall, soft stalks of golden grass that brushed his legs. As he looked back from where he had come, it appeared as if he had never stepped on any of the grass as he moved. When looking forward in the direction he walked it appeared as if the golden stalks moved away from his falling feet. He continued up a grassy foothill, looking for something or someone or nothing at all. At the top of the hill all he saw were more rolling hills in all directions and the golden stalks of grass blowing in the wind.

From the distance to his left he heard screams and what sounded like metal striking. He spun on his heels and witnessed two individuals fighting on an adjacent hill. He stood frozen for a moment and watched as the two lunged and parried. He felt he was watching a choreographed dance between two masters. Then one of the masters fell in an ungraceful manner that caused Lance to break into a run toward the performance.

Lance sprinted down the hill toward the fight faster than he thought he could and was unaware that his feet were not even touching the ground. As he raced to the top of the hill, he stopped only feet from the two fighters. One was a tall, silver creature and the other was a slender woman. The silver creature stood a head taller than the woman. Its limbs were long and muscular with each of its fingers as sharp as daggers. Its body was equally long and taut, with a smooth head devoid of ears. The woman wore a leather vest and a short, slitted skirt that hung high above her knees, but loose enough for her to move. Her long, auburn hair hung in her eyes and her muscles were chiseled and strong. Blood dripped from a gash in her vest above her right breast and sweat dripped from her nose. The silver creature turned its head to take notice of Lance and readjusted its fighting stance. The woman took the moment's glance to brush the hair from her purple-tinted eyes.

The silver creature lunged for the woman and slashed his long claws across her left thigh, drawing more blood. The woman did not waver. She brought the blade of her long sword down like an axe to cleave the creature's head. The silver creature dropped to one knee, raised both clawed hands, and caught the blade. Black blood dripped from the creature's palms as it used the ground to brace itself against the force of the sword. Using the sword as an anchor, the woman kicked the creature in the face. The force of the kick knocked the blade out of the creature's hands and threw the creature's head back in a forceful snap. The woman dropped the sword to the ground and pulled two daggers from their sheaths and lunged at the silver beast.

As the two blades of the dagger sank into the silver creature's shoulders, it threw its head back and howled in pain. As the silver body struck the ground from the momentum of her lunge, she pulled her blades out to stab it again in the chest. The woman lunged a second time for the beast's chest, but was backhanded across the face and knocked to the ground. The silver creature rolled on to its stomach and launched itself like a panther down the hill to flee the losing battle.

"Get back here, you coward!" the woman screamed as she rolled to her feet.

The silver creature quickly disappeared over the hills. The woman sheathed both bloody daggers and pushed her foot under the hilt of the sword and kicked it up into her hands. She sheathed her sword behind her back and turned to face Lance.

He knew her. He had seen her before. Here in this place. He didn't know where she came from. She was the first person he had seen here in this place in a long time. She had reached for his face, but then she was gone and he had woken up. He had seen her only for a brief moment. But that single moment left a lasting impression on him. He had spent many restless hours thinking about her. At one point he was tempted to call Dr. Mac and talk to him about this woman—about seeing people in his dreams again. But the more he thought about it, the more he decided not to call the doctor. Dr. Mac always believed him, at least he thought, but at times he wondered if the doctor thought he was just telling stories. In the end, he kept it to himself.

There was something about her that intrigued Lance. Of course he thought she was attractive, but it was more than a physical attraction. As dumb as it sounded to himself, that moment he saw her he felt a connection. A link. Maybe it was because she was in his dream? Maybe it was something else? Whatever the reason, he needed to see her again. He needed to feel that link again.

He had found her. He stood in front of this woman and wanted to ask her so many questions. He wanted to reach out and touch her. He wanted to feel that connection. He wanted to prove to himself that a link did exist. He opened his mouth to speak but was assaulted by a loud ringing sound. The sound was so loud he clamped his hands over his ears and fell to his knees. He tried to look at her, but all he wanted to do was silence the ringing sound. The ringing became louder and louder as each second passed. He could sense the woman stepping closer to him and he tried to look up at her. The pain of moving was unbelievable but he saw her purple-tinted eyes looking down at him in concern as she knelt toward him. Then his world went black.

XV

Ring.

Ring.

Ring.

Lance jerked awake with a start, "What the hell?" he asked out loud as he realized he was asleep and dreaming.

He looked toward the bedroom to see if his alarm clock was going off and realized it wasn't. He looked at his cell phone across the room and noticed it was dark, in sleep mode, like he should be. Lastly, he looked at the computer screen and saw that a call was incoming on Skype.

Lance leaned forward and pressed the answer key on the software program to end the annoying ringing sound. An older man's face with a salt-and-pepper beard and matching hair appeared on the computer screen. Lance thought Dr. Mac was looking more rested than normal.

"Good morning, Lance, or should I say good evening?" asked the Doctor.

Lance smiled. "I see you're sporting a beard now."

Dr. Mac rubbed at his furry chin and smiled. "Yes, I suppose I am. Just been too busy to shave I guess."

"So what are you doing up so late?" asked Lance. "And calling me? Don't you know I'm supposed to be asleep?"

"Well it's only a little past one for me," stated Dr. Mac.

Lance smiled. "That's still late."

"Well, in my line of work I steal as many hours as I can," justified Dr. Mac. "Plus I saw you were online and thought it was a good time to check on your progress. How have you been feeling?"

"Not too bad. My sleep attacks have lessened in number and I think the duration of each attack has gotten shorter," stated Lance as he tossed his manuscript on the desk.

"But obviously you are still not sleeping through the night," stated the doctor as he jotted down some notes.

"Hell, I never do," Lance said as he got up to make a bowl of cereal in the kitchen.

"Lance, since you have joined the center here at the university we have made tremendous gains…"

Lance interrupted the doctor from the kitchen as he poured the milk. "Whatever Doc, just don't feed me that bull crap about finding a cure," smiled Lance as he moved back to the desk shoving a spoonful of cereal into his mouth. "And no, I will not speak at any conferences," he finished with his mouth full.

Dr. Mac smiled and crumbled a piece of paper and asked, "So how's your love life?"

"Sucks." Lance hesitated. "Well, maybe not that bad," he modified.

"Care to expand?" pressed Dr. Mac.

"Not really."

"Humor me," pressed the doctor.

Lance swallowed his bite of cereal and let out a visible sigh of disgust. "You wouldn't have a love life or social life either if you fell asleep all the time," replied Lance. "It sucks. Why should I bother? I'd rather be a recluse and be known for my stories like Emily Dickinson was known for her poems."

"And may I point out that no one understands Emily Dickinson's poems because she was a recluse," interjected Dr. Mac.

Lance smiled. "There are some people who understand her specially crafted words."

Dr. Mac dismissed the rebuttal and continued. "I think you are holding out on me. I think there is someone in your life."

Lance smiled as he chewed.

Dr. Mac continued, "In either event, you were lucky that we caught your narcolepsy at such an early age."

"Ha!" snorted Lance through his milk-filled mouth.

Dr. Mac ignored him and continued. "If we hadn't, your love life or social life could be a hundred times worse, not to mention your overall health," finished the doctor.

Lance lowered the empty bowl of cereal, "Look Doc, you live with narcolepsy and see how it feels. I can't live a normal life. I fall asleep all the freakin' time, professors laugh at me, I can't keep a job, my peers avoid me like I have leprosy. So how the hell am I supposed to have a social life, let alone a love life?" asked Lance with the edge of irritability in his voice. Before the doctor could respond, Lance shook his head in apology. "Look, I'm sorry, just blame it on the lack of sleep." Lance smirked.

The doctor smiled understandingly and asked, "There must be someone you are interested in?"

Lance placed the palm of his hand on the camera of the computer to prevent the doctor from seeing his face.

"Don't ignore me, whoever she is, talk to her. I am sure she finds you fascinating," encouraged the doctor.

Lance dropped his hand from the camera in resignation, "Fascinating? Who the hell uses that word in the first place?" Before the doctor could make a comment, Lance continued, "I don't know, Doc. My whole life I have been a loner. I guess I just don't see the point.

"You've built some high walls, Lance; maybe it is time to let someone in," encouraged Dr. Mac.

"I don't know. Maybe," avoided Lance. Lance didn't want to tell the doc that he had asked Sophia to lunch just earlier that evening. He told himself that he didn't want to get the doc's hopes up. Or maybe he didn't want to get his own hopes up, he conceded.

Dr. Mac smiled and shook his head.

"I better go and try and get some sleep, Doc," said Lance, trying to end the call before the doctor gave him any more advice on his social or love life. Then he wondered when was the last time Dr. Mac had a social life or if he ever had one to begin with.

"One more thing before you go," commented the doctor. "I'm just curious—do you still see those silver creatures in your dreams?"

"Once in a while. But usually from a distance," answered Lance.

"No other details?" asked the doctor.

Lance shook his head no. He had stopped telling Dr. Mac the details of his dreams a long time ago. After one session he had a feeling that he shouldn't be telling Dr. Mac about the silver humanoid creatures he saw in his dreams. Not because he thought the doctor didn't believe him, but more because he was protecting something. Protecting an idea. He often thought he would turn his dreams into a novel or series of short stories. But for some reason he has never been able to record his dreams in a way that made sense in a story. Again, he thought it was his subconscious protecting some aspect of him or something with a higher purpose. His conscious mind wanted to tell Dr. Mac about his most recent dream, the dream about the auburn-haired warrior fighting the silver humanoid creature. But again it felt like his tongue was tied, even when he had the urge to articulate his thoughts.

Dr. Mac interrupted his thoughts. "Do you still see two moons at night?"

"Of course, every night since you've met me. Why?" Again, this was something else he regretted telling Dr. Mac. Not because he did not trust the doctor, but because it was a part of something larger that needed to be kept a secret from the rest of the world.

"Interesting," muttered Dr. Mac as he became thoughtful and jotted down a couple more notes. "I have some new experimental medicine that may prevent your hallucinations from transferring to your conscious mind while you are awake. The medicine might help you," stated Dr. Mac.

"Really, Doc?" questioned Lance. "You always dismissed me seeing two moons as my vivid imagination. Why the concern now after all these years?"

"I came across a reference," the doctor paused and hesitated to complete his thoughts, but continued. "There was a gentleman several hundred years ago that may have had narcolepsy." The doctor paused again. "Let's say his journal writings suggested the presence of a second moon," finished Dr. Mac.

Lance stared at the doctor through the computer screen for a long time. He could not figure out if the doctor was telling him the truth or trying to come at him from another angle. Finally, all he could think to ask was, "Really?"

The sight of two moons in the night sky every evening was something that always fascinated and scared Lance. In elementary school, when his class would study the universe and astronomy, he quickly learned not to ask about the second moon. When he did, it usually brought snickers and jeers from his classmates. When he talked to his mom and dad about it, they weren't much help either. His mom would just rub his head and tell him he had a vivid imagination and should be a writer. His dad took a different approach. His dad equated his ability to see two moons to being Superman growing up in a small Kansas town. His dad made him feel special, like he had a gift he needed to hide from the world until he was old enough to do something with it. For a kid, this was perfect. After the conversation with his dad he never talked about it again, except with his father.

Lance swallowed hard at the thought of his father. He missed him. He missed lying under the night sky and telling his dad what the second moon looked like compared to the only moon his dad could see. He missed sharing his dreams with his dad. No matter how fantastic or unbelievable his dreams were, his dad always listened and believed. The only advice his father ever gave him about his dreams was to not share them before he ate breakfast in the morning. This was advice passed down from his father's mother, who was part Native American. The American Indians believed that dreams came true if they were revealed before nourishment crossed the dreamer's lips. Therefore, no matter what time of day or night, if Lance had a dream to tell his dad, he always ate something first.

As a child growing up, he believed the ability to see two moons was a special gift, one that he cherished. Unfortunately, Lance told Dr. Mac about the second moon, the world of the purple sky and the silver humanoid creatures before his father told him to keep it a secret. He regretted telling Dr. Mac after he and his father talked. In some ways he felt that he had let his father down, even though they had not even had the conversation yet about keeping it a secret. So when Dr. Mac would bring up the reference to his secret ability, he would cringe. At those times he wished his ability to see two moons was a special gift, like one of the mutants from the X-Men might have, so he could prove to the doctor that what he saw was real. At those times and every day he wished he could talk to his dad again.

Dr. Mac interrupted his thoughts, "Yes. There was a reference to a purple sky and silver humanoids also."

"Is this a joke?" asked Lance.

The doctor looked genuinely shocked at the question. "Why would I joke about this? I believe you, just as your father did."

Lance shot the doctor a hard, stern look at the mention of his father, but then caught himself and relaxed his features. "Sorry," mumbled Lance. "What's his name?" asked Lance, not sure why.

"Whose name?" asked the doctor, confused.

"This other person. The person that wrote this journal."

Dr. Mac stared at Lance through the computer screen for such a long time that Lance almost started to think the Internet connection had frozen. But at the same time he got the sense that Dr. Mac didn't want to share the name with him. Dr. Mac made the motion of flipping through some papers and said as he looked away from the computer screen, "Gavin something. It is of no consequence."

Lance leaned forward and asked, "Gavin? Just Gavin?"

"Well Gavin something but I can't make out the last name," answered Dr. Mac.

Lance leaned back in his chair. Only his mother knew Gavin's name. One time he woke up from a dream and wanted to share what happened, but his dad was not around. So he told his mother. He told his mom about a man named Gavin who came to visit him in his dream. The man was telling him something about God's Liberators. His mom hushed him and told him that he had to stop watching soap operas. Confused by the comment, Lance asked his mom what she meant. She replied that Gavin was a soap opera name and not a real name. He never mentioned the name again outside of his dad's presence, not even to Dr. Mac. Maybe it was just a coincidence. But Lance had a difficult time believing in coincidences.

The doctor cleared his throat and Lance snapped out of his reverie. He focused on the doctor and asked in a curt tone, "Anything else, doc?"

Dr. Mac shook his head slowly with an appraising look. Lance could tell that he gave something away with his facial expressions and knew that Dr. Mac had picked up on his giveaways. He wanted to end the call as quickly as possible before the doctor asked any more probing questions. Lance knew he was no good at hiding information from Dr. Mac under close scrutiny.

"Try and get some rest, Lance," said Dr. Mac in a mechanical tone of voice. Lance could tell that the doctor was already lost in other thoughts and he just hoped it did not concern him.

"Good night, Doc," prompted Lance as he reached forward to move the mouse cursor to the end call button on the computer screen.

"'Night, Lance," said the doctor before Lance ended the call.

Lance pushed away from the computer desk and walked over to the sliding glass door to his balcony. He slid open the door and stepped out onto the cold wood of the balcony and looked toward the early morning sky. He crossed his arms over his chest and rose up on his toes as the first of the two moons set in the west just before the sun rose in the east. He thought about what the doctor had said and went back to the computer. He maximized the screen for his e-mail account and sent Sophia a quick note asking her if she wanted to meet for lunch later that afternoon. He yawned and pressed the send button. Before a second yawn could stretch his lips he lay on the couch and closed his eyes.

XVI

Dr. Mac leaned back in his chair and watched Lance's image on the computer screen blink out. He had the distinct feeling that Lance was keeping something from him. He admitted that in recent years Lance had not been forthcoming with information about his dream world. But this time it was different. Dr. Mac could tell that Lance was hiding something.

He pushed up from the chair and walked over to a large drafting table. Lying across the table were stacks of tracing paper covered with charcoal rubbings of some form of ancient text. Dr. Mac sat in the raised chair and reached for a stack of papers on the corner of the table. He leafed through the papers until he found the page he wanted.

***

Research Notes of Dr. James Mac

Journal Entry #34 translated from the "wall" text found in the tomb of Gavin Arbitor, circa 1110

They come from Toleous. A world far from ours. Dead before our time. They were forced to leave. They found our moons. They made one of them home. Hidden from our eyes. Hidden from our minds through our souls.

Their physical bodies have become useless. They need us to survive. In essence they are parasites. Parasites to our souls' energy. They feast on the weakened or confused soul. They cowardly attack the strong while they slumber.

They have mastered the art of astral travel. A technique unknown to our kind, save a few heretics. Heretics known as Shamans, Witch Doctors, Warlocks, Witches, and Magicians.

From our second moon these parasites I have named the Myst astral travel to our earthbound bodies. They sever the cords to our souls. A portion of our souls becomes lost to the aether. The other half stays trapped within our bodies. Death is the only way to free us from these parasites. Death of the human host. Through death our souls can begin again in a new life.

The gifted ones of our kind, the heretics, have been ridiculed and burned out of fear by fools. Through our slumber or meditations, we travel to the place with the purple sky. Here is where the heretics came to heal the sick of physical ailments as well as spiritual wrongs. This is the place where they met the spirits from the other side, the spirits who crossed over from life to death. Here they discovered the Myst. Here is where they learned that destroying the Myst released the trapped human soul to begin again. Here the strongest heretics became the Liberators. The Liberators of God's chosen people from the Holy Land.

The golden-eyed Myst are superior to their brothers. The golden-eyed...

***

Dr. Mac shuffled his papers and looked at the charcoal rubbings again. His eyes blurred. He needed a break. He walked away from the drafting table and peered out of his office window. He watched a young couple walk along the paved paths of the university holding hands. He instantly felt a pang of grief squeeze his heart. He missed his Norma. She was the light of his life. She brought him more joy than he ever knew could exist in the universe. She had brought him Sydney, their beautiful daughter. He missed her more than he ever knew was possible to miss a person. To his scientific mind it did not make sense. To his heart, it was broken.

He picked up the telephone and dialed a number. It rang three times before someone answered. A sleepy soft female voice asked, "Hello?"

Dr. Mac closed his eyes at the sound of his daughter's voice. "Hi, sweetie," he said almost in a whisper.

"Daddy!" exclaimed his daughter on the other end of the receiver.

The sound of the excitement in her voice brushed away the sadness that had enveloped his heart just moments before. She was like her mother in so many ways. Always excited to see him or hear from him. "I missed you," Dr. Mac said pointedly.

"I miss you too, Daddy. How are you?" she asked.

They spoke for several minutes about his research and his recent trip to Italy. She teased him for not bringing her along or bringing back a souvenir like he used to when she was a kid. At the end of the conversation he promised to visit her. But he knew it would be months before he could fulfill that promise. He told her that he loved her and she did the same. He returned to his drafting table with the stacks of paper and leafed through them with new energy.

XVII

Lance's cell phone rang from the other side of the room and awoke him from a deep slumber with a start. He scrambled across the room, grabbed the small black electronic box to look at the display. The screen was illuminated with a ten-digit telephone number and Sophia's name. He pressed the green telephone receiver button and put the cell phone to his ear. "Hey," he said as nonchalantly as he could, but he suspected that his eagerness was easily identifiable through his voice.

"Lance?" asked Sophia on the other side of the cellular connection.

Lance rubbed his hand through his hair. He looked at his sleep-consumed reflection in the mirror and turned away from the sight. "Hey, Sophia, what's up?" he said, hoping the remnants of sleep he still felt in his brain were not coming through in his voice.

"Hi, Lance, I was calling about the e-mail you sent me early this morning," spoke Sophia.

"Oh, great," said Lance as he moved his way over to the computer terminal and shook the mouse to eliminate the Darth Maul screensaver. "I thought you might respond with another e-mail," he said. In reality he preferred communicating through any means of written communication, which included letters, e-mail, or text, as opposed to speaking, because he felt his words flowed easier in printed form than as sound vibrations in the air. He often felt he could not find the right words to convey his message or the words turned into mutated vibrations as they traveled through the air and thus conveyed the wrong message. Plus he did not really have a lot of practice communicating verbally, considering he isolated himself from most of the world.

Sophia broke through his thoughts, "I did. But you never responded and it's getting close to lunch time, so I thought I would call."

Lance saw her unread message waiting in his inbox. Then he saw the clock on the computer screen and mouthed "Damn" when he realized it was fifteen minutes past noon. "Um, uh, well, I, uh," he said as he tried to think of an excuse why he had not gotten back to her.

Sophia laughed on the other end of the telephone call and asked, "You were sleeping, weren't you?"

Lance blushed and switched the cell phone to the other ear. "Um, yeah, kinda," he weakly admitted.

"It's okay, silly. Still want to grab lunch?" asked Sophia with a smile in her voice that he picked up on.

"Yeah, sure, where do you want to go?" asked Lance.

"Well, I'm allergic to wheat products so I'm limited on restaurant choices," admitted Sophia.

"You mean you're gluten-free?" asked Lance.

Sophia laughed on the other end of the telephone call. "Yeah, is that a problem, jerk?"

Lance smiled at the little jab. "No, not at all. Wheat is overrated anyway. I always feel bloated and gassy after eating a lot of bread or pasta." He paused when realized what he had said and blushed again. "I can't believe I just admitted to that," he defended himself as he smiled in spite of himself.

Sophia laughed. Lance realized he loved how easily she laughed. She skipped over the comment and said, "I know a great Chinese place across town," said Sophia. "How about if you meet me there in thirty?"

Lance calculated in his head how long it would take to get across town on his mountain bike and asked, "Actually, do you mind picking me up?"

"Of course, will fifteen give you enough time to wash the sleep away?" asked Sophia with a hint of a smile in her voice.

Lance chuckled. "Perfect."

"Okay, I'll see you in a little bit. Bye, handsome," said Sophia as she hung up the telephone before giving Lance a chance to say good-bye.

He watched the word "disconnect" scroll across the small screen and smiled at the thought that she called him handsome. He dropped the phone on the couch and peeled off his shorts and briefs as he moved into the bathroom. In the bathroom he grabbed his daily medication and swallowed the pills as the water in the shower heated up. He jumped in the shower for a few minutes to wash his hair and body. He quickly dried off and threw on a pair of jeans and a light blue shirt with Captain America on the front. He started to yawn, but shook his head to fight off the sleepiness that threatened to invade his consciousness. He slipped on a pair of Columbia flip-flops and then the doorbell to his apartment rang.

Lance glanced at the door in disbelief and quickly looked around the small living room and kitchen area to make sure all the dirty clothes were picked up and nothing inappropriate was lying about. When he determined the apartment was clean and no incriminating evidence was visible, he opened the door with his hoodie in his hands and greeted Sophia with a huge smile. "You're early."

"I was eager to see you; it's been a couple weeks since we shared coffee," replied Sophia as she stuck her hand out to shake his.

Lance looked at her hand and chuckled. "What's that?" he asked.

Sophia looked at her hand and back to his eyes. "A handshake."

Lance smiled. "You're funny. Come here," he said as he opened his arms and gave her a hug. Sophia hugged back and Lance realized her hug was longer and more firm than just a regular friendly hug. He smiled.

The hug ended and Lance closed the door and they both walked down the hall to the elevator. Sophia had started down the hallway before Lance and gave him a chance to soak in what she was wearing. He figured she probably looked great in anything because it was obvious she kept herself in shape. But there was something about her presence that simply made her beautiful. He caught up to her at the elevator and said, "You look nice today."

Sophia turned and looked at him and smiled. "Thanks," she said with a slight blush, and turned away to avoid eye contact. She pressed the down arrow key for the elevator and asked, "Do you like living alone?"

Lance smiled. "Let's just say I have an allergic reaction to roommates."

"Doesn't it get lonely?" asked Sophia as the elevator doors opened.

"Honestly, no. I like my own company." He stopped and thought about it a little bit more. He knew he could use narcolepsy as an excuse for why he lived alone, but he knew that was not the real reason. He took a deep breath and remembered Dr. Mac's advice. He did have high and thick walls to protect himself. He glanced at Sophia and smiled. Maybe it was time to let someone behind those walls. "I'm not like most people. I can handle sitting in silence for hours at a time and think nothing of it. I can keep myself entertained by working out, riding my bike, reading, writing, or thinking of new ways to dominate the world," he finished with a smile.

As the elevator moved down each floor Sophia asked, "What do you write?"

Lance looked at his feet, "Ramblings mostly. I like to tell stories, so that's what I do. I sometimes write technical stuff and poems."

"That's really cool," reassured Sophia.

Lance looked at her as the doors of the elevator opened on the ground floor. "I guess. I've never been published, but I keep trying. Sometimes I think I like rejection and that's why I keep trying."

Sophia looped her arm through Lance's and led him out of the elevator and through the lobby of the apartment complex to her car. "Maybe you just haven't found the right audience yet."

Lance looked at the profile of her face and knew that she was using all of her self-control not to look at him in return. He smiled so hard that his cheeks hurt.

"I usually order chicken fried rice with no onions. What about you?" asked Lance.

"Me too. Can we share?"

XVIII

Cora sat in the coffee shop, slightly hunched over the small circular table, with her book opened in front of her. Occasionally she would reach out and take a sip of her coffee. If someone asked her what her favorite genre of books was, she did not think that she could answer that question. She knew she hated romance novels, probably as much as she hated country music. She did enjoy true life stories: survival stories of men and women overcoming the odds. She was also attracted to Holocaust stories. A friend once told her that she might have been a survivor of the Holocaust in a past life and that is why she was drawn to those types of stories. Whatever the case, she was not interested in her book that evening. She was more interested in the crowd of people around her.

Normally Cora would never hang out in a coffee shop alone. But for some reason that night she was compelled to grab her book, get a cup of coffee, and just lounge. Her book just wasn't grabbing her attention. She enjoyed watching the four older men in the corner playing dominoes more than anything else. She also watched the bald-headed man across from her typing on his laptop. She thought he was cute and kept hoping he would glance her way. But he looked very intent on finishing whatever he was writing. She heard the grind of coffee beans behind the counter and then smelled the aroma. She groaned to herself and realized that she was going to smell like coffee the rest of the night. Cora frowned at her coffee and wondered how she could forget the number one reason why she hated coffee shops to begin with. She hated to smell like coffee.

Cora closed her book and stood up from the table. As she looked up a man in his mid-thirties with long, blonde hair walked past her toward the exit. As he moved past, Cora caught the reflection of the man in the mirror. It was not the man's reflection—it was a Myst. The name came to her one night in a dream. It made sense. So she started using the term in reference to the silver creatures she killed. As the man pushed through the door he turned and looked back at Cora. In the reflection of the mirror the Myst turned and looked at her with a slight evil grin spread across its lips.

Cora felt momentarily dizzy. She gripped the table to balance herself. Every instinct in her body screamed out for her to chase the man down. She hesitated. Was that real? Did that really happen? she asked herself. She sat back down at the table. She ran her hands through her hair and pressed the palms of her hands tight against her eyes.

She thought to herself, Those are only in my dreams. They aren't real!

"Oh my God, I'm going crazy?" she said out loud. She looked up from her table. The four older men were still playing dominoes and the bald-headed man still typed on his computer. They looked normal. Everyone in the coffee shop looked normal. She watched half a dozen more people walk in and out of the coffee shop past the same mirror and she saw each of their reflections. Leaving her unfinished coffee on the table, Cora grabbed her book and walked to the mirror. She saw her own reflection. She saw her auburn hair, her purple-tinted eyes, and her cream-colored skin. She reached out and touched the mirror to make sure it was real. In her mind's eye she saw the Myst reflection again and its little grin. A voice inside of her head whispered, It's stalking you.

XIX

Lance and Sophia held hands as they walked down the busy city sidewalk in the crisp, cool night. It had been a few weeks since their afternoon date to the Chinese restaurant, but tonight felt like their first official date. It was one of those nights where fall could not determine if it was ready to let winter take over or continue to fight for its last days of cool weather and falling leaves. The sidewalk was busy with families and couples walking in and out of stores and restaurants, determined to take advantage of fall and winter's inability to make a decision. As Sophia and Lance maneuvered through the crowd of people, refusing to release their grip on each other, they talked about nothing and everything. Their words came easy and their laughs were continuous throughout their conversation. Lance liked the feel of her slender fingers between his and wished he could hold her hand all the time. His attraction to Sophia had been growing each day since they shared lunch together. However, because of his disability, he still felt shy around her. He was having a hard time believing that she was equally attracted to him. He wished and hoped that her feelings for him were as strong as his were for her. He feared that she would not let herself feel that way because of his narcolepsy.

A majority of the time they were together he was able to stay awake and not fall asleep. But there were a few times he dozed off. Usually it happened when they were watching a movie, or sitting in traffic, or lying on a blanket at the park. When he awoke he was always embarrassed. She always had a smile on her face and was gently petting him. When he apologized she laughed at him and said apologizing was unnecessary and that she understood. She also teased him that she liked to watch him when he slept. He felt a little embarrassed that she watched him, but it also reassured him. The only other person who ever watched him sleep was his mother. He always knew his mother watched while he slept and that always made him feel safe and protected. He felt that way with Sophia also.

Lance looked at Sophia and smiled and pulled her close to him to give her a quick kiss on the lips as they waited to cross the street. After they crossed the street, Sophia took the lead and turned down a side street that looked more like an alley. Halfway down the alley was a small sign illuminated with yellow lights that read Madam Zerlynn: Seer of True Love.

Lance stopped and tugged Sophia's hand to a stop. She turned back to look at him, "Really?" asked Lance with a smile.

Sophia stepped toward Lance and twisted his arm behind his back without letting go of her grip on his hand and pressed her body against his. "Yes," she whispered as she kissed him on the lips.

"Is this your way of seeing that we are compatible?" asked Lance as he continued to feel his body against hers.

"No silly, I already know that," Sophia responded.

"Oh," he whispered.

She untwisted his arm and walked to the glowing sign. The door to the establishment was old and worn, with no windows. Over the entrance of the door hung several strands of beads that were pulled back like a set of drapes and the base of the door frame looked as if thousands of people had walked through it. Lance doubted that even a hundred individuals had sought out Madam Zerlynn's advice on true love. Sophia turned the door knob and pushed the door open, "You first."

Lance stepped over the threshold of the door and immediately felt that something was wrong. He hesitated long enough that Sophia actually gave him a little push on his back to scoot past him and close the door behind her. As the door closed, he looked around and noticed that not much was in the room. One large mirror hung on the wall to his left, a circular table with three chairs was positioned in front of the door they had just entered, and directly across from him and Sophia was another entrance hidden behind a beaded curtain. Hanging over the center of the table was a chandelier holding twenty to thirty blazing candles.

Sophia glanced at Lance and felt his hesitation and took his hand in hers. She leaned toward him to kiss him on the cheek and whispered, "You okay?"

"Uh, no. Not really," said Lance as the feeling of uneasiness continued to wash over him.

Lance glanced over at Sophia and saw her standing next to one of the chairs waiting for him. He tried to smile and crossed over to the table as calmly as he could. He sat down in the chair next to hers. Sophia sat next to him and touched his hand. "What's wrong?" she asked.

Lance looked at her and tried to smile bigger. "Nothing. Just being paranoid I guess," he said, squeezing her hand. He looked away. "Maybe I'm afraid you'll learn my deep, dark secrets."

"You can't scare me away, Mr. Juddit," said Sophia.

At hearing his surname, Lance looked at Sophia and chuckled. "Where is she?"

Sophia leaned in close to Lance's ear and whispered, "She's behind the mirror watching us," as her words left her lips Lance had to close his eyes to focus on the sound of her words because the feeling of Sophia's warm breath against his ear sent chills and sparks through his entire body.

When she finished speaking, he whispered in her ear, "I wouldn't do that again," and gave her ear a quick gentle lick before moving his mouth away. He glanced at her face and it looked as if his words and actions had frozen her face with a devilish grin.

He smiled and looked up at the chandelier and saw that at least seven of the candles were unlit and swore three more puffed out when Madam Zerlynn walked through the beaded curtain doorway and stood behind the single unoccupied chair left in the room. The soothsayer was older than Lance expected. He was expecting the soothsayer to be in her sixties. She appeared to be closer to her nineties, but he suspected that was impossible. She wore a long flowing dress with multiple patterns and colors covering every inch of the fabric. He figured the dress was chosen to hide her large size and equally large breasts. Her silver hair was in a loose bun gathered on top of her head and her face was lined with wrinkles around her eyes and lips, but also across her forehead. The most curious thing Lance saw was a faint silver outline of a thin body within the soothsayer's large form. He tried not to stare at the woman's face and the silver glow that emanated from her. He turned to look at Sophia to see if she noticed anything unusual. Lance could tell from Sophia's facial expression she was not seeing the same thing he saw.

"You wish to see the future?" asked Madam Zerlynn as she sat in the last chair. The weak wooden chair squeaked in protest, trying to support the woman's weight.

"Yes," said Sophia as she reached for Lance's hand under the table.

"Very well, may I start with you?" asked Madam Zerlynn as she turned her attention toward Lance.

Lance sat up straighter and clutched Sophia's hand harder. "Why don't you start with her?"

The old woman looked at Sophia and back to Lance, "No, I have a feeling about you," said Madam Zerlynn as she reached for his hands. "Give me both your hands."

Lance glanced at Sophia to try to boost his courage, but only felt more apprehension flow through him. Lance reluctantly stretched his hands across the table toward Madam Zerlynn's. Even though she was a large woman, her hands were slender as if she had pulled on human wrinkled leather skin gloves over a skeleton's hands. As she turned his hands over Lance could still see a faint silver glow radiating through her skin.

Madam Zerlynn started to speak in a low, soft voice. Lance was unable to comprehend what she was saying because a disturbing thought struck him. The silver glow within her skin reminded him of the creatures he saw in his dreams—the silver creatures he dreamed of as a kid and the silver beast that mysterious woman fought in that golden field of grass. The thought did not make sense to him; those were just dreams. He then remembered how Dr. Mac believed that him seeing two moons was a by-product of his dreams. Was this the same thing, he wondered?

Madam Zerlynn pulled him from his thoughts when she instructed, "Look into my eyes."

Lance blinked for a long time before looking up and meeting her gaze. Madam Zerlynn's eyes were a magnificent light green color with specks of gold and small black pupils. He wondered how her pupils were so small in such dim lighting. But as he looked into her eyes, he watched as the pupils of Madam Zerlynn's eyes changed from black to silver.

Lance felt his body lean closer toward her as if he was being pulled into her eyes. He felt as if he was losing control of his own actions and thoughts under her intense stare. Images of his dreams and reality started to mix together in his mind the longer he was mesmerized by her eyes. Lance felt afraid that he was losing himself to Madam Zerlynn. He didn't understand how that was possible. He forced himself to break eye contact and pull his hands away from Madam Zerlynn's.

The old woman howled in disgust when the contact was broken. Lance glanced toward the mirror on the wall and saw a reflection of a silver humanoid creature sitting in Madam Zerlynn's chair.

The soothsayer yelled at Lance in an angry tone, "Why did you break contact?" as she lunged across the table to grab his hands again.

Sophia slapped the woman's hands away and yelled, "Back off, bitch," and turned to Lance asking, "What's wrong?" as she grabbed his hands.

Lance flinched and tried to pull his hands back from Sophia's touch. She held firm. He looked at Madam Zerlynn and could tell she was not happy. He looked at Sophia, who looked confused. "I'm sorry, I can't do this."

Sophia tilted her head to make eye contact with Lance's downward gaze. "Do you want to leave?"

Everything in Lance's body wanted to scream Yes! Instead he shook his head and said, "No, I'm okay. Just got spooked. I'll be okay."

"You sure?" asked Sophia again.

Lance tried to smile at her and squeezed her hands. "Really, I'm okay. Your turn, sweetie."

Sophia gave him a half-hearted smile and turned her attention to Madam Zerlynn. Madam Zerlynn was still visibly upset. Her breathing was labored and she struggled to bring it under control. She gave Lance a long, hard look before taking Sophia's hands and started the same ritual with her. Lance noticed the pupils of her eyes were black again, but once Sophia looked into the woman's eyes they shifted to silver again. Lance focused on every detail and word that Madam Zerlynn spoke to try to figure out what had freaked him out so bad. The soothsayer mumbled useless words of advice about good health, love, and prosperity and then Lance saw movement in the corner of his eye. He looked up toward the mirror on the wall and watched a second silver humanoid creature emerge from behind the beaded curtain and enter the room. The silver creature slinked around the table past Madam Zerlynn toward Sophia.

Lance sat up straight. He looked to the beaded curtain and watched as the strings swayed in a breeze he did not feel. He glanced back to the mirror to see where the silver creature was and then back to the room where it should be standing. All he saw was Sophia and Madam Zerlynn. He slowly stood unnoticed by the two women. He looked back at the mirror and saw the reflection of himself, Sophia, and two silver humanoid creatures. The feeling of dread he felt when he first walked across the threshold struck him like a kick to the throat when he saw Madam Zerlynn staring at him with silver eyes. He could feel the hatred of her wrath coming at him from her icy gaze.

Lance felt the second silver creature hiss in his mind and he looked toward the mirror. He watched in horror as the thing lunged at Sophia. Sophia threw back her head and screamed in agony. Lance quickly glanced between Sophia and the mirror. Watching in the mirror he witnessed the silver creature evaporate into a gaseous mist. As he looked back to Sophia he watched in horror as the mist seeped into Sophia's eyes. Sophia's limp body collapsed, causing her to slam her head onto the old wood of the table. Lance finally reacted. He felt a fiery rage surge through his body that gave him more strength than he realized. With one hand he pulled Sophia off the table and back against her chair. With his other hand he flipped the heavy wood table onto Madam Zerlynn. The chair Madam Zerlynn sat in was unable to support the weight of the woman and the table and gave up its effort. The chair, the old woman, and the table all collapsed on the ground in a loud crash. The soothsayer screamed in pain and anger at the turn of events.

Sophia awoke from the sudden jerk of Lance throwing her back in the chair and Madam Zerlynn's loud scream. She felt blood trickle down her forehead and then found Lance's hand in hers.

"Come on!" yelled Lance as he pulled Sophia from the chair.

As Lance raced toward the door he caught a quick glimpse in the mirror and saw the silver creature of Madam Zerlynn leaping through the wooden table at him. He raced through the door with Sophia in tow and did not stop running until they were blocks away from Madam Zerlynn's.

XX

Cora stood on a rock formation hundreds of meters above the waterfall that descended into the Oasis of Calm. Her feet were bare and wet from the water spraying off the Dark River. She looked down at her vest and fingered the tear above her right breast from her previous battle. The wound had healed, but she forgot to mend the leather torn by the Myst's claw. She unbuttoned one more button on her vest, showing more cleavage than necessary, and ran her hands over her breasts and down the front of her damp skirt. She checked her many daggers and sheathed sword before running her wet fingers through her auburn hair, pushing it back over her scalp. She squatted and waited. They were coming and she could feel it.

Cora did not have to wait long as two Mysts appeared on the edge of the Oasis of Calm. One appeared and then the second one hesitantly appeared next to its partner. When they appeared, she squatted down on her haunches at the top of the rock formation to hide from their sight. They appeared to be in conversation. The second Myst seemed nervous or anxious. Cora thought that was odd because she never saw any other emotion except hatred from these creatures. The two Mysts talked for a long time, almost as if the first one was giving directions to the second one.

Cora waited and watched. Then they both started to climb the rock formation above the Oasis of Calm. Cora watched as the first one climbed up toward her, almost as if it knew exactly where she was hiding. The second Myst curved off to the right and climbed within meters from where she was hiding. She'd faced worse odds before and survived. Barely. She slowly moved closer to the ledge to get a better angle to watch the two creatures and maintain her slight advantage of higher ground. Unfortunately, the first Myst saw her. Its arms and legs grew longer and it climbed faster to reach the summit of the rock formation. Cora stood and backed away from the edge. She waited.

The Myst slowly slinked over the edge of the ledge toward her. Across the open gap of space Cora could see the drool from the Myst's fangs as they grew more pointed. Its fingers grew longer and sharper as the bloodlust increased within itself in anticipation of the battle. From its ledge, the Myst paced back and forth, waiting for the right moment to attack. The second Myst crested the ledge and advanced toward Cora without hesitation. Any sign of anxiety was clearly gone from the creature. Cora crouched down on her haunches, waiting for the attack that could come from either side.

The first Myst on the ledge took two long strides and launched itself through the air to confront Cora. Cora waited and watched as the creature flew through the air, its claws outstretched, ready to penetrate her skin. She waited to spring in the air to meet the attack. However, the attack never came. In mid-air the Myst vanished, disappearing from the confrontation. Cora sprang to her feet with a rush of anxiety and dread. She knew it was gone, but only temporarily. She hated how the Myst could come and go from this world with such ease. For her it was a curse and a blessing to be here. A curse because she had to fight these creatures and a blessing because she had been given a chance to destroy them. She never understood why the Myst simply vanished. She suspected there was a relationship between its host being awake or asleep. But what about the Myst who did not have a human host body, where were they? Or did they all have host bodies?

A low growl snapped Cora out of her thoughts and focused her attention on the second Myst that strode toward her. When its partner had vanished it paused. Its original anxiety and hesitation returned to its face. Cora dropped back into a fighting stance, hands raised to protect her face, legs spread apart for a strong base. The Myst extended its neck and head toward Cora and released a primal scream in defiance at her. Both fighters started circling one another, waiting for the other to strike. Cora watched the eyes of the Myst and sensed its fear. She anticipated an easy kill; this one was not the fighter of the two.

Cora attacked first. She threw a punch with her left fist toward the Myst's chest, knowing it would be blocked, to be followed up with a drop to the ground and a sweeping dragon-tail kick to the thin legs of the creature. Her punch never got blocked. As the punch got close to the creature and the creature moved to block the punch, the creature was violently thrown backward by an invisible force. The

Myst went over the edge of the rock formation. Cora pulled her punch and ran to the ledge and looked over.

The Myst held onto the edge of a rock above the waterfall. With a pull of its long arm, the Myst propelled itself up onto the ledge. Cora turned and leapt to another rock formation and retreated from the battle. Something strange was happening and she knew this was not a time to fight. Cora knew she would have to avoid any other confrontations until she woke up again in her reality. She hated to run, but she fled.

XXI

Sophia pulled on Lance's arm and stopped him in the middle of the sidewalk yelling, "What the hell is wrong with you?"

"I am sorry Sophia, it was just…" Lance trailed off in silence.

"What is it?"

"Please, not here. Can we go back to my place," he urged as he pulled Sophia's hand to follow him.

"What's bothering you?"

"Things like that scare me. I just flipped out. I'm sorry," he said as he realized her forehead was still bleeding. Lance used his sleeve to wipe the blood off of Sophia's face.

"Okay," said Sophia as she wrapped her arm around his when he was done cleaning her bloody face. They turned and started walking back toward his apartment.

XXII

Lance sat on the couch, looking out the window of his apartment with his hands wrapped around a cup of tea Sophia had made. He sat quietly thinking about the images in his mind and what he saw at Madam Zerlynn's. He thought to himself that maybe he should call Dr. Mac. But what would he say to him? He would sound crazy telling Dr. Mac that silver humanoid creatures were jumping out of people's bodies and walking around in mirrors. Hell, Dr. Mac would probably call the authorities and have him committed at a mental health facility.

His dad. He would call his dad. His dad always believed him. His dad never thought he was crazy. Lance looked at the time and saw that it was just past eight in the evening. He might still be able to talk to his father. He called out to Sophia, "I have to make a call real quick." Before she could answer him he jumped up from the couch and walked out onto the balcony. He pulled the sliding door closed behind him. He took a deep breath and dialed his father's number. The telephone rang on the other end until a female voice answered. "Hi, can I please speak to Mr. Steve Juddit?" asked Lance. The female voice on the other end of the telephone asked him to wait. He impatiently waited. Then he heard his father's voice.

At the sound of his dad's voice, Lance already started to feel more relaxed, "Hi, Dad."

"Otis, is that you?" asked Mr. Juddit.

Lance dropped his head and sighed into the telephone, "Yes, it is your brother Otis," responded Lance with resignation in his voice.

Excitedly Mr. Juddit responded. "How the hell are you?"

"I'm great, Steve. How are you?"

"Oh you know, same shit. Diabetes is killing me, but at least that damn boulder didn't get me in those mines," answered Steve. "You remember that don't you? I was working in those mines."

"Yes Steve, I remember," answered Lance.

"Hey, do you remember that time up on the hill with, um, shit, what was his name?"

Lance leaned against the railing of the balcony and looked up at the two moons in the evening sky. "I love you, Dad, and I miss you," spoke Lance.

"What's that? Luthor? Hell no, that wasn't his name. Oh whatever, I have to go anyway. Great to hear from you. Send my love to Linda," said Steve and hung up the telephone.

Lance looked at his cell phone and then back into the night sky. He swallowed hard and willed the tears back into his eyes. He opened his eyes and patted his chest twice with the palm of his hand.

Lance pulled the sliding glass door open and joined Sophia on the couch. She had made herself comfortable by wrapping a homemade blanket around her shoulders. Lance sat next to her, pushing his hip into hers. "Who did you call?" she asked.

Lance stared out the sliding glass door. "My dad."

"Why?"

Lance looked at Sophia and thought that was the stupidest question he had ever heard in his life. He looked away and took a deep breath to calm his nerves. Maybe he was just tense from what had happened earlier in the evening. He looked at the two moons and said, "I just needed to hear his voice for a second." Lance paused. "I miss him, and he has a way of calming my nerves. Well, he used to, at least."

Sophia looked over at Lance. "Where does he live?"

"Not far, about a twenty-minute bike ride," said Lance.

Sophia smiled, "Oh you must get to see him a lot then?"

Lance thought for a long time before answering, "I do. Weekly."

Sophia frowned and then smiled, "Well it's sweet that you miss him even though you see him every week."

Lance looked from the two moons to Sophia, "You don't get it. He has dementia. He doesn't remember me." Lance paused to try and push the lump down in his throat, "He hasn't remembered me or my mom for years."

Sophia pressed her legs tight against his. Lance made no effort to move. She watched him for a few seconds as he stared out the window. She picked up her cup of tea and sipped it quietly. Leaning her shoulder against his, she asked, "What do you see?"

"Two moons," he replied.

Sophia looked from the night sky to Lance and then back to the night sky and asked, "Are you feeling okay?"

"Tired."

"Do you see two of anything else?" asked Sophia with concern in her voice.

Lance turned his head to look into Sophia's eyes. "No. But it sure would be fun to see two of you," smiled Lance, trying to make light of the situation. He wanted to tell someone so bad what he had seen that night. He wanted to share with someone what he experienced every day. But as soon as he spoke the words that he saw two moons to Sophia, he regretted it. His inner voice told him that she was not the one to tell. She was not the person he could trust to keep that secret. At that moment he chose to ignore his inner voice.

Sophia grinned and nudged Lance hard with her shoulder and they both attempted to dance their tea cups in the air to not spill a drop. Sophia leaned over and kissed Lance softly on the lips. Lance asked her, "You don't believe me about the two moons, do you?"

Sophia looked out into the night sky. "It's not that I don't believe you, I just don't see it."

Lance looked out to the night. "The second one is slightly higher and to the right of the moon you see." Lance watched as Sophia's eyes tracked in the direction he said. He could tell that she did not see it. "It looks very similar to the moon you see. I'm sure the craters are different, but it is darker and it appears to be slightly smaller than your moon."

Sophia looked at Lance and leaned her head against his shoulder. Lance took a sip of his tea. Sophia asked, "Are you teasing me?"

"Dr. Mac thinks it's a leftover hallucination from my subconscious when I fall into one of my narcoleptic sleeps," said Lance, ignoring her question.

"Do you believe that?"

"Sometimes I would like to believe that, but in reality I don't."

Sophia put her cup of tea down on the table and laid her head on Lance's lap in order to look up at him. Lance placed his tea down and played with her dark hair. Sophia asked, "You think it is something else?"

"I know it is something else." He looked out at the night sky before continuing and then back to Sophia. "Every night, my second moon rises and sets with your moon." He looked out at the moons again. "The second moon isn't the only thing that I see that others don't."

Lance waited and hoped for the Like what? to cross Sophia's lips for him to continue. Instead she turned her head to look out the window again and said, "I wish I could see your moon. I bet it is a beautiful sight."

Disappointed, Lance yawned and watched the two moons climb higher in the night sky.

XXIII

Cora lay on the track with her hands behind her head and looked up into the night sky. The two moons shone bright against the tapestry of stars. She eased her breathing to a calm and steady pace. She felt her body sweat out the impurities from her run. The night air felt good on her bare skin and helped relax her mind. She looked up at the second moon that she knew the rest of the world could not see. The heavenly body that she knew only she could see in the night sky. She never told anyone about the second moon after the night her house burned down and her mother disappeared. After that night she lived with aunts and uncles. She never mentioned the second moon nor the place with the purple sky and the Mysts. Something inside of her warned her to never share that information with anyone outside of the Seekers for the Liberators and she never did. She often wondered what happened to the Seekers. They vanished along with her mother. She tried looking for them in hopes of finding someone from the group. She had fantasies that if she found a Seeker, she would find her mother and would therefore find answers to the questions that plagued her. After several years she quit looking. It was useless. The Seekers were gone, just like her mother. Still, Cora could remember times when she wanted to tell someone so badly about the second moon. As she got older the sense to keep it a secret felt more like a duty to keep silent. So she did with pride. However, like tonight, she often wondered if the rest of humanity would ever see the beauty of a twin moon rising.

Cora assumed the second moon would remain hidden from the sight of common men just as they knew nothing of the Myst. She often wondered how the people she passed on the streets knew nothing of what happened in their subconscious as they slept at night. Over the years she had tried to find evidence through research that a second moon existed or that humanity knew about the Myst. She had come across references in pagan religions that believed a second moon named Lilith existed, Lilith being Adam's first wife—the wife Christian-based religions hid from the rest of the world. According to pagan beliefs, Lilith refused to be subservient to Adam. Basically, she refused to lie under him when they made love. She was replaced by Eve and banished to the second moon, which was called the Dark Moon of Lilith. Astronomers in the seventeenth and nineteenth centuries documented the existence of this moon, but modern technology failed to prove that the second moon was real—which made Cora believe that a higher force or intelligence was hiding its presence from humanity. Her guess was the Myst. The Myst were somehow responsible for hiding the second moon from human consciousness by blinding the connection to the universal consciousness that all human souls possessed.

In all of her searching she had never found a reference to the Myst. Many metaphysical authors and speakers had referred to silver creatures in their dreams. Fantasy and science fiction authors had written about alien life forms similar to the Myst, but nothing referring directly to the Myst. Cora admitted that some writers had come close. Still, no one understood the truth. She had even tried to contact authors, asking about their sources for stories or references closely related to the Myst. The authors never wanted to give away their Muse.

Cora's thoughts drifted to the stranger she encountered on the World of the Purple Sun. She wondered if he happened there by mistake—or if he was one of those metaphysical or fantasy writers that was lucky enough to tap into their subconscious? Or someone who opened his mind through meditation just enough to accept the impossible? Or was it possible that it was her time to step aside from the battle and let this new one continue the fight?

Her guess was that he was familiar with the World of the Purple Sun. From her perspective he appeared to be at ease in that place. The feel of his energy belonged to that place, as if he belonged there, as if he was originally from that place. His presence did not make sense to her. Then again, a lot of things that happened in her life did not make sense to her. She shook her head in disagreement with herself. She decided that he was not from that world. He was from hers because it was clear to her that he could come and go as he pleased. Just like her.

"I wonder if he sees the Dark Moon of Lilith?" she asked out loud. He must, she thought. If he could come and go as he pleased from that world, then he must be able to see the two moons in the night sky just like her. Who is he, she thought? More importantly, where is he? She wanted to know.

Cora pushed off the ground from the track and jogged home, smiling. She no longer felt alone. She did not know where he was, but in her heart she now knew that someone else in this world saw what she saw.

XXIV

On the other side of the country, Dr. Mac lit a new candle in his office after the second one of the night had burnt itself out. His family had a tradition of burning a candle when it was a loved one's birthday. Today was Norma's birthday. Even though she had passed away several years before, he burned a candle for her on their anniversary and her birthday. He had loved her very deeply in fact. When the darkness crept into her body and took her away, it took part of him also. If it was not for their daughter, Sydney, he would have lain down next to his Norma and joined her. Sydney was his life preserver. She did not know, and he vowed she would never know, how close he was to joining Norma during those dark times. She, his precious daughter, kept him on this side of the light.

He turned his attention to a package he had received a few days earlier from an archaeological dig in southern Italy. He used a letter opener to tear open the package and pulled out a note and several pieces of rubbing paper folded together. The letter was short and to the point.

Dear Dr. Mac:

As you know the archaeological community has been aware of your search for many years. My students came across the enclosed Latin inscription in a tomb in the southern portion of Italy. We have taken the liberty to translate the Latin for you. We hope this is helpful in your search.

Sincerely, your colleague,

Dr. Seed

Dr. Mac carried the fragile rubbings to his workbench and unfolded them carefully. He admired the beautiful rubbings the students had made. He lightly traced his fingers over them, trying to feel their origin in the skin of his fingertips. In some silly way he hoped a thought or an image of the past would enter his mind through the rubbing of the inscription. His rough fingertips traced over a group of words that jumped at him and caused him to stop in wonderment: the Latin words Duae lunae.

Dr. Mac whispered to himself, "Two moons." He walked over to the window and looked out at the night sky at the one moon he saw and whispered, "Lance." He quickly turned back to his drafting table and leafed through his stack of papers that contained the translations from the text written on the wall of Gavin Arbitor's tomb. He found what he was looking for and read the excerpt again with new interest.

***

Research Notes of Dr. James Mac

Journal Entry #79 translated from the "wall" text found in the tomb of Gavin Arbitor, circa 1110

I am hidden from the world for fear of being a demon! I rise from the dead and I speak of things that are impossible. I see things that others do not or fear to see with their eyes. I am hunted by those of my own kind. I am hunted by peasants who fear that I talk of two moons in our celestial skies. I am hunted by those who seek to cease my liberations of our brothers and sisters against the silver beasts in my dreams. How they know who I am and what I do in my dreams is unbeknownst to me.

I am no demon! I am a man in Christ! I am a man blessed by God to liberate his children from the evil that threatens our existence in the world he, our Creator, has made for only us.

We, the liberators before and after me, are the only human creatures our Lord the Creator made that can see the blessed two moons in the celestial skies above when slumber has passed. For our lives we must forever stay silent of our perception of the physical world around us and our dream travels.

***

Dr. Mac pushed away from his drafting table and pulled a file off of his computer desk. He opened it and peered down at a photograph of Lance. He glanced through the clinical notes and easily picked out the references to a second moon, silver creatures, and a place with a purple-tinted sky. He flipped back to Lance's picture and mumbled to himself, "I knew you were special."

XXV

The leaves smacked Mr. Boggs in the face, waking him from his sleep. He looked around at his surroundings and saw hills of golden grass rolling for miles under a velvet sky. Occasionally, he saw giant trees with thousands of silver leaves reaching for the clouds. As he watched the golden grass and the silver leaves, they seemed to sway and bend to the power of a wind he could not feel.

"Where the hell am I?" asked Mr. Boggs out loud as he pushed off the ground to stand up. He looked around and rubbed his wrists, wondering how he got to this beautiful place. He saw a speck of a bird fly overhead in a wide circle and wondered if he was alone. Instinctively he knew that he was not alone. A feeling of dread and fear crept into his mind and he tentatively looked around again, searching for something menacing to jump out at him and attack.

Reluctantly, but knowing he needed to move, he slowly waded through the tall golden grass. As he passed the trees he wearily looked up into the branches for any sign of trouble. As he crossed over the third hill, the last of the trees disappeared and all he saw were more golden hills of grass rolling in the distance.

Mr. Boggs continued to cross over each golden hill and lost count of the number of hills he traversed. As he crested the next hill he saw a stream at the bottom. Realizing that he was thirsty, he quickened his pace to the bottom. He reached the stream and kneeled to the clear water. He submerged his hands into the coldness.

"Over here," whispered a voice on the wind.

Mr. Boggs jumped from his kneeling position and looked around for someone—but saw no one. Instead, he saw only the golden grass sway and the shadow of the bird that seemed to be following him. Mr. Boggs dismissed the voice as his imagination and kneeled to the water again.

"Over here," whispered a voice on the wind.

Staying in his crouched position, Mr. Boggs looked around for the voice. He stood up, crossed the stream, and started up the next hill.

"Over here," whispered the voice on the wind again.

Mr. Boggs started to run. Reaching the top of the hill he stopped quickly before falling off the edge. He looked over the edge and saw a wild river with jagged rocks and rapids, the distance to the bottom unimaginable, the pain of falling there unthinkable. Mr. Boggs took a step back from the edge and looked out to the horizon.

"Right here!" screamed the voice on the wind.

Startled by the loud voice, Mr. Boggs jumped without thinking. He watched the ground zip past his face and realized he was over the edge. In desperation, he clawed at the air helplessly.

At the top of the cliff a man dressed in a black-hooded cape walked to the edge and peered down to the wild river. The man in the black-hooded cloak watched as a stream of white and silver mist drifted off into the velvet sky.

"Your soul is free to begin again, Mr. Boggs."

XXVI

Cora leaned against her broadsword and watched as Mr. Boggs fell to his death. She was not bothered that another human soul was released. She was bothered by the nature of the death. In all of her battles she had never killed a human directly in their dreams. She had always confronted the Myst directly. Never the person. The concept made sense to her. If the person died in their dreams, they would be released from the bondage of the Myst. Still, it did not settle well with her.

Cora pulled the sword from the ground and sheathed it behind her back. Her movement caught the attention of the man in black. She felt him staring at her. She knew who he was. Her fingers twitched at the memory of his energy when she touched him.

He stood across the gorge from Cora, peering at her from under his black hood. She was tempted to propel herself across the gorge to confront him. She did not, for fear of giving away a talent that he may not have been aware that he possessed in this world. He pulled his hood back and let the wind blow his black cape. Cora could see the outline of weapons against the man's body. At first glance she could see two wooden hilts protruding over his shoulders, strapped to his back. The outside of each boot had a dagger strapped to it and several other blades hung on his sides and across his chest. Impressive, she thought. But does he know how to use them in a fight? Then he pulled the hood back over his dark hair and turned his back on Cora and glided down the hill away from her.

Clearly he has learned how to manipulate this world and his actions within it, thought Cora. Was what he did a show to her of his mastery of this world? Or did he disregard human life in a way that allowed him to kill the person directly and not the Myst? Her fingers twitched again at the memory of his energy. No, he must not have mastered how to see the silver beasts apart from the person. Her thoughts were broken when she heard a faint whisper on the wind: "Lance."

XXVII

Lance opened the curtains to let the morning sunlight shine in through the living room windows. He gave himself a second to enjoy the sight of the sun and the morning warmth. In the adjoining kitchen, Sophia stood over the stove wearing his old high school shirt. She was making breakfast for the both of them. The entire apartment was filled with the sound of fat sizzling in the frying pan and the smell of bacon and eggs. He stared out at the brightness of the day and thought about his dream. He remembered only bits and pieces of his dream. He remembered wearing a black cloak, the warrior woman with auburn hair, and a man falling from a cliff. He remembered feeling responsible for pushing the man off of the cliff. But it was necessary. It was necessary to purge the man from the evil that lived inside of him. To liberate the man's pure soul that was trapped in his human body. Sophia broke through his train of thoughts by asking, "Whatcha' doing over there?"

Lance turned from the sliding glass door and watched as Sophia took a sip of her coffee. "I was thinking about the dream I had."

"What was it about?" asked Sophia.

Lance crossed over to the kitchen, "Um, I can't tell you," he said before continuing. "Not until I eat first."

Sophia laughed and asked, "Why?"

"My father was part Native American and he said if I told anyone my dream before I ate, it would come true. And to be honest with you, I don't think I want this dream to come true," answered Lance.

"Well, in that case, how do you like your eggs?" asked Sophia as she smiled at Lance.

"Scrambled and the bacon burnt," Lance responded as he crossed the kitchen to give Sophia a hug from behind at the stove.

Sophia poured the eggs into the skillet and checked the bacon as Lance held her with his head on her shoulder. She turned around to face Lance and pushed a piece of hot bacon into his mouth. "There, tell me about your dream now," smiled Sophia.

Lance chewed and smiled at Sophia at the same time. He let go of her and slid over to the coffeepot. He swallowed the bacon. "It was about a man being pushed off of a cliff," Lance said as he poured his coffee. He paused for a moment and watched Sophia fidget with the hem of his shirt. "I don't remember being in the dream, but I knew what the man was thinking and the fear he felt when he was dying. The strange thing is, I think I was responsible for his death." Lance paused and decided it was best to keep the part out about the warrior woman with the auburn hair. If Sophia questioned him about that he would not know what to say. So he just decided that part of the dream was not important for Sophia to know about.

Sophia turned to check the eggs and used a spatula to scramble them. She removed the bacon from the stove and reached for two plates from the cupboard. "Sit down, breakfast is almost ready." Lance watched Sophia move throughout the kitchen and wondered why she had not commented on his dream. He even started to wonder if he had actually spoken the words out loud or just in his head. Sophia caught his eye and finally said, "That's interesting."

Momentarily stunned, Lance went over to the kitchen table and pushed his school papers to the side. "Let's watch the news and see what's going on in the world," said Sophia as she turned on the television with the remote control.

Sophia brought Lance a plate full of eggs, bacon, and toast. She placed her plate diagonally from his and joined him at the table. They both ate and listened to the news in silence.

From the television an aging news anchorwoman interrupted the scheduled broadcast to announce a special bulletin report, "Arms Committee Chairman Congressman Edward Boggs was found dead in his Vermont vacation home this morning. Authorities believe Congressman Boggs died from a heart attack while he was asleep at approximately 5:30 this morning. More details will follow as the story develops," said the news anchorwoman.

Lance instantly got sick. He dropped his fork and quickly ran from the table toward the bathroom and vomited in the toilet. Sophia sat at the kitchen table and waited until he was done vomiting before she got up to see if Lance was all right. She went into the bathroom, wet a washcloth with warm water, and wiped his forehead with it.

"I always thought I was a pretty good cook," said Sophia as she rubbed his back and handed him the washcloth. Lance could not figure out if she was trying to be funny or if she was being serious. He looked at her face and he could tell that she was trying not to smell or look at the vomit in the toilet. He flushed the toilet.

"No, he was in my dream last night," Lance said as he wiped his mouth clean.

"Who was in your dream last night?" asked Sophia.

"Congressman Boggs. He was in my dream last night." Pausing to catch his breath, he turned to look at Sophia. "That was the man that was killed last night. He was the one in the dream I was telling you about."

Sophia stepped back from Lance and dropped her hands by her sides and rubbed the side of her thighs. "So now you are telling me that you can predict the future?" asked Sophia as she walked backward, placing distance between them.

"No, I am not saying that. I remember saying in my dream something like, 'Your soul is free to choose again.' Then I awoke and

I recall seeing what time it was, and the clock said a quarter past five in the morning."

"But first you told me you weren't in the dream? So what are you getting at?" asked Sophia as she moved out of the bathroom and toward the kitchen.

"The reporter said that his approximate death was at 5:30 this morning from a heart attack. In my dream I frightened him." Lance paused. "I mean the man in black frightened him and he fell off a cliff. Maybe the fall in his dream is what caused him to have a heart attack."

"What man in black? You didn't mention anything about a man in black. Were you the man in black?" asked Sophia as she moved to sit on the couch.

"No," paused Lance. "I mean I don't know."

Lance sat next to Sophia on the couch. "Maybe you were able to witness his dream and his death," she offered.

"Are you suggesting that I am able to enter into people's dreams?" Lance asked.

"Maybe?"

"I don't know," Lance said as he reached out to hold her hand. "But now I am thinking I was the man in black but didn't realize it at the time."

"Okay, that is weird," said Sophia. "Why were you the man in black? As in the Grim Reaper or something?"

"Hell, I don't know. The whole dream in itself was weird," said Lance thinking back about the dream. He closed his eyes and replayed the events in his head again. "I mean maybe, but if you are suggesting that I was the embodiment of the Grim Reaper, then are you suggesting that I killed Congressman Boggs?"

"Killing someone in your dream doesn't make you guilty," assured Sophia as she squeezed his hand.

Lance thought to himself, The man in black felt like me.

Sophia was looking past Lance, thinking about something. She turned her gaze back to Lance. "You said that you saw a silver inset in Madam Zerlynn's body."

"Yeah, that's right."

"Did you see anything like that in your dream?" asked Sophia, not really expecting an answer.

"I don't remember."

Sophia leaned closer to Lance and gave him a kiss on the cheek. Sophia got up from the couch and pulled her hand out of Lance's. He noticed that her fingernails were painted silver. "Where are you going?"

"I need to go home and get ready for class. It's almost 7:30, and I have class at 9:00," she said as she picked up her slacks from the living room floor and headed for the bathroom.

When she came out of the bathroom Sophia had changed back into her clothes except for his shirt. She grabbed a piece of toast from his plate and gave him a quick kiss on the cheek. "I'll call you later."

"Okay," Lance said as he watched her walk to the front door. When she opened the front door the daily newspaper fell into the doorway. Sophia bent down and picked up the paper and turned to walk back into the kitchen.

"You could have just left it there on the ground," Lance said.

"I want the obituary section."

"Why?"

Sophia got an embarrassed smile on her face, "It's one of my weird hobbies." She reached across the table and stole a piece of bacon and turned to walk away again. Lance pulled his knees to his chest and rocked slightly back and forth, trying to comfort himself. This time she waved without looking and closed the door behind her. When he heard the lock of the door click he collapsed into a fetal position on the couch and began to sob uncontrollably. Eventually he fell asleep.

XXVIII

Lance stood on the hiking trail that opened up to a large field in the middle of the forest. The trail cut through a large swath of golden grass that lead to a dead end against a jagged rock cliff. The tree line of the forest arced in a semicircle around the field to the same rock cliff. In the middle of the field was a semicircle of large stones. He had the distinct feeling that the stones were burial markers but he was unsure why he felt that. He looked up toward the blue sky over the forest that merged with the purple sky above the field.

He knelt and rubbed his hand over the loose dirt of the path. A few feet in front of him he saw what appeared to be a footprint. Lance stepped across the threshold of the forest into the field to examine the footprint more closely. He traced his pointer finger around the outline of the print. It was a large print with a heel, five toes, and no visible arch. It was leading into the forest away from the field. He looked back toward the forest, but continued down the trail deeper into the field.

As Lance walked farther down the trail, the golden grass extended higher toward the sky. Eventually the tree canopy of the forest was hidden from view. Lance hesitated and wondered if he should continue or turn back. As the thought crossed his mind, a gentle breeze blew through the golden grass. Through the breeze he felt the soft hum of a voice drift across the wind.

"Enter," hummed the wind.

Lance slowly spun in a circle looking around and up toward the purple sky. The wind hummed again, "Enter."

He continued to turn, not sure of what he was searching for, and then saw the cave. As he made his frantic circles looking for the source of the whispering wind, the golden grass had parted to reveal the opening of a cave in the rock cliff not far from where he stood.

Lance knelt down to examine the cave. The opening of the cave was so small that he could barely squeeze his shoulders into it. With his head just in the entrance of the cave he could see nothing but blackness.

Lance closed his eyes and took a deep breath. With the inhalation of this breath he crawled deeper into the cave. The darkness consumed him as it consumed every inch of the cavern. He crawled on his stomach and strained to see a light at the end of the tunnel, but saw none. The darkness fed his desire to find an exit. A fleeting thought crossed his mind to retreat to the golden grass field and the forest, but he also felt that retracing his steps was not an option.

The darkness grew denser and more frigid, with no end in sight. Lance rested his forehead on his outstretched arms for what seemed like hours, but he knew it was only a few seconds. When he lifted his head from his arms he saw the edge of the tunnel cave looking out into a desert. He reached out toward the sand and scooped up a handful and sifted the grains through his fingers. He used both hands to pull himself out of the cave onto the desert floor. He looked toward the sky and saw a purple sun and the landscape of a dry desert.

As he stood, Lance peered down at his feet and saw they were covered in black leather boots. He outstretched his arms and saw his hands and forearms were covered in black leather gauntlets. A dagger was strapped to the outside of each calf. Over his chest he wore a black leather vest with two daggers attached to his sides. His legs were covered in black, flexible leather and around his waist was a belt that held a short sword on his left hip and a black pouch on his right. He felt a black cape wrap around his leg and held the cape up with both hands to examine the strange metal-like material. Lance reached over his head and felt two wooden handles. He unsheathed the weapons and held two short swords in front of his face.

"What the hell?" said Lance out loud. "Oh, I know I'm dreaming now."

Out of the corner of his right eye Lance saw movement on the desert floor. He turned to look and watched as a shiny silver tiger raced toward him. It sprang into the air as it leapt from the top of a sand dune. At the height of its jump, the beast twisted its body into a downward dive toward the sea of sand, and shapeshifted into a tall, silver humanoid. The Myst landed on two feet with an impact that shook the ground.

The alien extended its claws and advanced toward Lance without a hint of reservation. Lance turned to fully face the alien and instinctively took a step backward. He bent his knees and staggered his stance for better balance. He lifted one sword over his head and the second sword in front of his chest. Without hesitation the Myst leapt in the air. The alien extended its long body out over the sandy ground, stretching its long arms and claws toward Lance. Lance waited and spun in a circle away from the alien at the last possible moment. Lance brought his left arm over his head down across the alien as it passed him in the air. When Lance quit spinning, his right arm still held the sword across his chest and his left arm extended behind him with the sword dripping with black blood.

The Myst dropped into a forward roll and disappeared in the sand, leaving one arm lying on the desert floor. Seconds later the Myst reemerged from the sand with only one arm—but with a partner. The partner was slightly shorter and stockier, with its tongue licking its long fangs.

The shorter of the two Mysts released a howl of challenge that broke the silence of the desert. The attacking Myst used its arms like an ape to propel its charge toward Lance. The Myst was closer than Lance expected when it leapt and used both feet to strike Lance in the chest, knocking him several feet backward before he hit the ground. Lance dropped both swords.

The Myst pounced on Lance and straddled him. The alien struck Lance hard in the chest and grabbed his head to smash it to the ground. Lance struggled to reach his two daggers attached to his boots. The Myst bent forward with its mouth open wide to sink its fangs into Lance's face. Lance grabbed both daggers, pulled them from their sheaths, and stabbed the creature in the buttocks before its fangs ripped open his face. The Myst let out a painful scream. Lance shoved with all of his strength to topple the creature. When the alien landed face-first in the sand, Lance leapt from his position to land on top of it. On his knees, Lance stabbed both daggers into the back of the creature's neck. The Myst fell limp against the sand and dissolved under Lance's body.

The one-armed Myst kicked Lance in the back of the head before he was able to stand. Lance fell face-first in the sand while the alien lashed out with its claws at his back. The alien clawed at the cape and tore it to shreds. The one-armed Myst grabbed Lance's head and lifted him off the ground and tossed him to the side. Lance struggled to his feet. The one-armed Myst spun in a lightning-fast circle and ripped open Lance's stomach with two of its claws. Lance buckled in pain and felt the Myst grab his head again. He watched as it kneed him in the face. Lance landed on his back. He could feel blood dripping from his nose.

Lance screamed in frustration and anger. He pushed himself to his feet. With nothing to lose, he rushed the Myst. Lance sped across the sand toward the alien creature. Before he reached the Myst, he dropped to one knee and used a dragon-tail kick to knock the Myst's legs from under itself. The Myst collapsed on its back. Lance brought a stiff arm down across the creature's neck and used both hands to grab its silver, bald head. For a moment Lance looked into the black eyes and then broke its neck. The Myst melted into the sand under him.

Lance looked at his empty hands in surprise. His hands began to shake. His whole body shook. He pushed off the ground and stood. He looked around and saw no evidence of the fight. Both remains of the Mysts had vanished. The only thing he saw different was two silver streams and two white streams of vapor float into the purple sky. He whispered, "May your souls be free to begin again." He did not know why he said it, but it felt right and necessary.

He wiped the blood from his face and walked over to his swords. He picked them up, examined them, and wondered where he had learned how to fight like that. He had taken one self-defense class his entire life and he never learned how to fight with a sword or even how to kick. He sheathed both swords and daggers. In the distance he saw some trees and wondered if they were the same trees from the forest path. Probably not, he thought, but he moved in that direction.

As he moved toward the trees, Lance concluded that he was dreaming. Only in his dreams would he wear all black leather with a cape, know how to fight like a sword master, and win against a pair of aliens. When he neared the trees the heat that rose off the sandy ground began to shimmer. A form of a man appeared in the shimmering heat. The man wore long purple robes that wrapped around his body. He stepped from the shimmer and Lance immediately recognized him as Gavin Arbitor, the man who used to visit him in his dreams when he was a child.

Gavin bowed his head—"Lance"—as a form of greeting.

Lance froze in place and stared in disbelief. "Are you real?"

"Yes and no," replied Gavin.

"What the hell does that mean?" asked Lance.

"Many years ago I inhabited a body like yours, but now I am just a spirit."

"A ghost?"

Gavin shook his head no, "A spirit. I am one of God's Liberators." He paused as if he was gathering his thoughts. "I am your spirit guide. I am a brother in arms. I inhabit your dreams to guide you. You were chosen by God to liberate human souls from the Myst."

"What? You live in my dreams?" asked Lance.

"Yes, brother. If you think back deeper in your mind, you will come to realize I have been in every dream you have ever dreamt. I am your guide in this battle against the Myst." Gavin reached out and grabbed both of Lance's shoulders. "You were chosen by God before you were born. All of God's Liberators were chosen before they were born. We were each blessed with a gift. You were blessed with the gift that allows you to walk through dreams. Only you can end the pain of the Myst that began so long ago."

Lance stood in the hot sand and looked down at the black, tattered robe that danced around his body. He understood what Gavin said but he did not understand how or why. All of those moments in his life when he felt like he was being groomed or prepared for something greater fell into place. Gavin's words resonated within Lance's soul.

Gavin continued. "Everyone's dreams are different, and they have different beliefs. Therefore, you will take on many shapes, forms, and names. You will learn how to control your mind, your shape, and your own dreams." Gavin raised his arms above his head and spun in a circle, showing Lance the world around them. "Remember this is your dream world, this is your battlefield, this is what you control."

Gavin repeated, "Remember this is what you control."

The heat waves from the sandy ground began to rise behind Gavin. Gavin took a step back into the heat and his image became a blur to Lance. Before Gavin disappeared, Lance heard Gavin's voice one more time. "If you look hard enough in each dream you will see me, brother. But I fear the time has come that the Myst have dropped the veil of secrecy and are becoming bolder. At least in an effort to destroy you in the physical world."

A roar broke the silence as a beast of unimaginable size crashed through the forest and charged Lance. Lance dropped back into a fighting stance and awaited the attacker. The beast mutated into a Myst and lunged at Lance. Lance made a sidestep to the creature's left and extended a stiff-arm strike across the long throat of the silver alien and knocked it to the ground. Lance did not hesitate. In one motion he unsheathed a sword from his back, dropped to one knee, and sliced the Myst's neck with the blade. The Myst's body sank into the sand as soon as its body went limp. Lance shuffled away from the open sinkhole and watched as a silver mist and a white mist rose from the sinkhole into the deep vastness of the purple sky.

Gavin's voice spoke from the trees. "The soul is free to begin again."

XXIX

Lance lay on the couch for hours, asleep in a fetal position. Once in a while he would moan or kick his legs. Otherwise he was still. Although his eyelids remained closed, his eyes flicked violently underneath. The sweat from his body drenched through his clothes and onto the couch beneath him.

Unbeknownst to Lance, Sophia quietly entered the dark apartment and headed toward the bathroom. She gathered Lance's medication and walked back into the kitchen. She poured a glass of water and knelt down to Lance to brush the hair from his face. Sophia spoke softly as she caressed his face. "I am sorry I left you here by yourself all day."

Another hour passed before Lance awoke from his narcoleptic sleep. As his body jerked awake he tried to sit up quickly but felt a pair of hands push him back down to the couch. Feeling his head land on something soft, but firm, Lance looked up and saw Sophia smiling down at him.

"Lie here and relax for a minute. Here's some water."

As Lance took the glass from Sophia, his hands shook while he tried to drink. He sat up on the other side of the couch so that he could get his bearings. He stretched his neck and looked around the room to make sure he was back in his apartment. The dream with the Myst and Gavin was still vivid in his mind.

Sophia reached for Lance's hands and clasped them both in hers, pulling him toward her lap. "I am sorry I left you alone all day."

For the first time, Lanced noticed that her eyes were a combination of two colors, green and silver. In the center of her eyes was a silver starburst with hints of green erupting from the pupils. The longer he looked into her eyes, the more he felt as if he was being sucked into the silvery green starbursts of her eyes like what had happened with Madam Zerlynn. Trusting Sophia, Lance leaned closer as if to kiss her but continued to see the images of creatures and places dance across her eyes that were all too familiar to him. They were reflections of a purple sun, enormous rock peaks, tall silver bipedal creatures, an earth with two moons, and humans with silver skin. He did not understand why he was seeing these images in her eyes. These were his memories. His dreams. How did she possess them? He continued to watch as the images flashed by faster and faster, getting larger and larger as they continued to consume him.

Lance tried to pull away from her gaze but was unable to break free. Still staring into Sophia's eyes, Lance saw a tiny, silver speck grow larger, as if moving toward the surface of her eyes. The silver speck began to take shape into a two-legged creature with an elongated torso and limbs. In a blinding instant a Myst leapt through Sophia's eyes at Lance. Instinctually, Lance pulled back in fright and yanked his hands free from Sophia. He fell off the sofa onto the floor.

Lance was not sure what was happening. Something pounced on him and pinned him to the floor. When he focused his eyes he saw Sophia, but at the same time flashes of the Myst. He struggled to get away. The Sophia-Myst had him pinned down with its arms and legs. As he struggled, the silvery presence of the alien encased Sophia's body. She or it—he could not tell anymore—held him down with unbelievable strength.

The Sophia-Myst moved its head and eyes closer to Lance. Its head turned from side to side as its eyes peered into Lance's eyes. With all of his willpower he tried to close his eyes, but it felt as if something was stretching his eyelids open. He struggled to turn his head. He was unable to move. A silver mist started to seep out of Sophia's eyes and drift down toward Lance's face. The silver mist wrapped around Lance's head like a fog and started to crawl over the ridges of his eyelids and behind his eyes. Lance screamed as loud as he could when he felt the silver mist penetrate his body. Not only could he feel the physical presences of a foreign entity in his body, but he could feel the white essence of his soul fighting against this foreign invasion.

Lance pulled back within himself in an effort to try to protect his soul. As he concentrated on the inside of his mind and soul, his outward fight with the Sophia-Myst faded. Lance briefly wondered how someone could protect their own soul. How does a person strengthen his or her soul against the Myst invading his or her body? Through willpower? Through the power of the mind? Through God?

Lance stopped struggling. In his mind he imagined himself sitting down cross-legged in a field of tall golden grass with a purple sky. The silver vapor from the Myst still swirled around his head. He struggled to control his breathing. He counted each inhale and exhale. Each breath was slow and controlled, each inhale and exhale the same duration. He softly began to sing: "Blue skies and rainbows and sunbeams from heaven are all I need when the Lord is living in me." The Myst pulled back. Lance sang it louder. "Blue skies and rainbows and sunbeams from heaven are all I need when the Lord is living in me." He felt his soul swell with pride. The song became a chant to Lance. "Blue skies and rainbows and sunbeams from heaven are all I need when the Lord is living in me."

In his mind's eye, he sat under the purple sky in the golden field of grass. He saw the head and body of the Myst form in front of him. He could feel the silver mist retract from under his physical eyes. He reached his hands up and shoved as hard as he could. The silver alien let out a loud, piercing shriek of protest and the remaining silver vapor burst out of Lance's eyes. The alien creature lay limp in the golden grass. Lance stood with blood dripping from his eyes and whispered one more time: "Blue skies and rainbows and sunbeams from heaven are all I need when the Lord is living in me."

***

Lance awoke sometime later. His body was stiff and sore. His head and eyes hurt. He was afraid to move and afraid to open his eyes. He searched his mind and soul for any trace of the Myst within him. But, he wondered, how he would know? A mirror? He wondered if he was possessed, would he see the silver alien in the mirror like he did at Madam Zerlynn's? Then he concluded he would not be having this conversation if he was possessed.

Lance opened his eyes and looked up at the ceiling of his apartment. He half expected to find himself staring at a purple sky. He was relieved to see the boring white ceiling of his living room. He pushed to a seated position and that is when he saw Sophia lying a few feet from him, sprawled over an overturned chair. Lance tried to quickly crawl over to her. His aching body protested with each movement. He finally managed to pull his sore body close enough to see her face. Her eyes were burnt black. Dried blood lined her face down to her chest and covered most of the floor around her. There was no need to check if she was alive. He knew she was dead. Nevertheless, he pushed his fingers against her neck. Nothing.

He backed away from Sophia and hurried for the door. Lance leaned against the doorframe for support and looked one last time at Sophia. He did not want to leave her dead body alone, but he knew he had to go. He did not think he was leaving out of fear. He knew he was leaving out of survival. Before he turned and left he whispered, "Your soul is free to begin again."

He dragged himself down the hall, using the walls for support. Once he got to the stairwell he collapsed down the four flights of stairs and crashed through the exit. In the dark alley Lance lost his balance and fell into a row of trash cans and boxes. He lost consciousness and his world went black.

XXX

Dr. Mac parked his car in front of the Narcolepsy Research Center at the university and walked up to his office. As he entered, one of his assistants handed him a stack of papers and Mark rushed up to meet him. Dr. Mac could tell he was a bit frantic.

"You have a call on hold waiting for you. I've been trying to reach you all morning," stated Mark.

Dr. Mac pulled out his cell phone and saw that he had four missed calls. "Sorry, guess I didn't hear it ring."

"I know. Books on tape. Anyway, the woman is waiting," repeated Mark.

"Woman?" wondered Dr. Mac. He hurried to his desk and picked up the receiver. He pushed the hold button to take the call. "Hello, this is Dr. Mac."

The female voice on the other end of the line announced herself, "Hello James, this is Grace, Grace Juddit."

"Grace, what a surprise," exclaimed Dr. Mac.

"James, I wish I was calling under better circumstances. But Lance is in the hospital."

Before Dr. Mac could react, Grace continued. "He's in a coma. He was found in an alley behind his apartment complex. The doctors have no idea what happened, nor do the authorities."

Dr. Mac sat and leaned back in his leather chair. He let out an audible exhale. "Grace, I'll be there immediately."

"Thank you," whispered Grace as she hung up the phone.

Dr. Mac leaned forward to his desk and hung up the telephone. He dropped his face into his hands and rubbed them over his balding scalp. He took a deep breath to try to calm his nerves. He knew he was in shock. He never wanted to admit it, but Lance had always been the closest thing to a son that he ever had. He needed to be by his side for professional and personal reasons.

Mark knocked on the door and entered Dr. Mac's office wiping his hands clean with a paper towel and took an uninvited seat in the doctor's office. Dr. Mac said nothing. He leaned forward with his forearms resting on the desk.

"Sir, you okay?" asked Mark.

Dr. Mac did not answer. He just stared at Mark and could tell the young man was unsure how to continue. He could tell that his graduate assistant had important things to tell him. He wondered if he appeared as rattled as he felt.

"James, this morning has been rough." Before Mark could continue, Dr. Mac shot him a look of anguish. Mark hesitated, but continued. "We have gotten several calls this morning that several of our patients have died."

Dr. Mac closed his eyes and stood up from his chair. He walked over to the office window. He pulled open the blinds and looked out the window at the college campus. I wonder how many students have a sleep disorder that goes undiagnosed.

Mark cleared his throat and continued. "Doctor, these reports span the whole globe."

Dr. Mac continued to stare out the window. Without turning to his graduate assistant, he stated, "Mark, I need to go east for a few days."

Mark stood up in protest, "But sir—"

Dr. Mac turned around and held a finger up to silence the student. Mark turned on his heels and left the doctor's office with the door swinging closed behind him.

XXXI

Cora stood on the rooftop of her building and admired the beauty of the two-moon night. The cool, brisk wind blew through her auburn hair as she started to trace the perimeter of the building with her footsteps. At each corner she leaned over the edge to see the gargoyles that sat perched just under the roof's ledge. At one time she guessed there were at least four gargoyles, one for each corner. But for reasons unknown, only two were left. She felt safe here. She believed the two gargoyles watched over her and protected her. Over the years she had lovingly named them Grumly and Bozz. She did not know why. The names just seemed to fit their personalities. She smiled at the thought. Every stuffed animal she ever had, she named. She believed all things had a personality, a soul.

Cora sat against the north ledge of the building between the corners where Grumly and Bozz sat perched. She needed to find the man in the black cloak. She needed to find Lance. Since her last encounter with him, she had argued with herself on the pros and cons of finding him and connecting with him. She admitted to herself she was attracted to him, more because he could fill the void of isolation she had felt her entire life as opposed to his physical characteristics. Cora also needed to find him because she had awoken earlier in the evening with a sense of dread surrounding him. He was in danger. She knew without a doubt he needed her help. She prepared herself to meditate. She touched the leather pouch with the black cat remains that hung around her neck and concentrated on her breathing. After a handful of breaths she opened her eyes and saw the air before her shimmer into a haze. Through the shimmering air she could see the World of the Purple Sun. She felt the physical sensation of her soul pulling away from her physical body. There was a slight tug and her awareness drifted before her corporeal body. With her soul eyes she glanced back at her body and followed the soul thread that attached her spirit to the physical world. She turned back to the shimmering air and stepped through into the light of the purple sun.

***

Lance dove in the air and tackled the Myst in mid-flight. He pressed his knee into the alien's back, forcing it to the ground. With his left arm, Lance grabbed the alien's eye sockets, pressing his fingers deep into its black holes. The creature jerked its elbow back and caught Lance above the left eyebrow. His eyebrow tore open, spilling blood onto the sand. Lance held his dagger in his right hand and slashed the creature from the corner of its lip through the cheek, past its ear. The Myst's body went limp and collapsed to the ground when Lance released his hold.

As the Myst disappeared under Lance's knee, a silver mist and a white mist drifted into the velvet sky. Lance whispered, "Your soul is free to begin again."

***

Cora stood in the hot sun and watched as Lance ripped open the Myst's mouth. She sensed that he hated what he just did, but he appeared to be so confident in his actions. She drew her sword and held the hilt with both hands in front of her.

Lance lifted his head when he heard the metal of the sword scrape against its sheath. His actions were slow and deliberate, Cora sensed. He stood and wiped the blood of his dagger on his pant leg and slid it into the boot sheath. He turned around and saw her poised in front of him with her sword drawn. He opened his hands to show that he was unarmed. She already knew that he was unarmed, but it was a nice gesture. He asked, "Who are you?"

Cora countered, "The question should be, who the hell are you?"

XXXII

Dr. Mac stood in the doorway of the hospital room and watched for a moment as Grace sat by her son. Looking up at her son, she rested her head on his leg. Lance lay still in the bed with several machines and an IV attached to his right arm. He was breathing on his own and his eyes flickered violently under his eyelids. Dr. Mac walked into the room and placed his hand gently on Grace's back to let her know he was there.

"Are you okay, Grace?" asked James.

Grace raised her head and sat up in her chair. She took her free hand and wrapped it around James's waist and pulled him close to her.

"James, I'm so glad you came."

James could hear her muffled cries against his shirt. He held her for a few minutes to let her cry as he watched Lance lie in his coma. James pulled Grace to her feet and let her lean against him as he walked her out of the room.

In the hallway Grace wiped the tears from her eyes and cheeks as James grabbed a handful of tissues from the nurse's station. "Grace, have the doctors told you anything?"

Grace took the tissues and blew her nose, shaking her head no. "They don't know anything. He can breathe on his own. One doctor seems to think that he is stuck in a cycle of REM sleep."

James sat down in one of the chairs against the wall. Grace joined him. He took off his glasses and rubbed his eyes. "Yes, I can see that he is in a REM state." He put his glasses back on. "How did they find him?"

"They found him in the alley behind his apartment complex. One of his neighbors heard some noise and went over to his apartment to make sure he was okay. The neighbor found his girlfriend Sophia dead in the living room." Grace wiped the fresh tears off her cheeks. "They called the police and they found him unconscious outside."

James wrapped his arm around Grace's shoulders and pulled her close to him. "Do they know how Sophia died?"

Grace sniffed and blinked her eyes, "No." She blew her nose again. "Only visible signs were that her eyes were burnt black."

"What?" asked James, confused. "You said her eyes were burnt black?"

Grace nodded her head yes.

Before James could ask another question an alarm went off in Lance's room. Grace and James hurried into the room, followed quickly by a nurse and doctor.

Blood drained from Lance's left eyebrow as he lay in his bed. His right fist tightly squeezed the bed sheets. His eyes danced wildly under their lids. The nurse immediately applied pressure to the cut on his eyebrow while the doctor checked Lance's vital signs.

Grace wrapped her arms around James. "What's going on, James?"

Before James could answer her question, Lance violently kicked the footboard of the bed.

XXXIII

"I don't know," answered Lance.

"What do you mean you don't know? Are you sick in the head or something?" asked Cora with a trace of irritation.

Lance tried not to smirk, "My name is Lance."

Cora eyed Lance and offered her name. "Cora. At least you know that much."

"Thanks," offered Lance. He looked around the desert landscape and back to Cora. "I thought I was the only human who came here. Or knew how to come here."

Cora relaxed and sheathed her sword. "I know what you mean. How do you travel here?"

"I fall asleep," replied Lance.

"What?"

"I have narcolepsy. So I fall into an uncontrollable sleep from time to time. When I sleep I come here," answered Lance. "How do you come here?"

"I meditate," answered Cora.

Lance looked at her, "Hell, I wish I had that gift."

"It's not a gift," countered Cora defensively.

"Sorry, didn't mean to offend you. I just assumed that it was. Gavin said that we each had a unique gift, and I assumed yours was meditation. I assume with meditation you can control when you come here and when you leave. Me, I have no control over my comings and goings. I have a disability, which somehow is a gift," said Lance.

"Who is Gavin?" asked Cora.

"You don't know who Gavin is? I just assumed you knew who he was because you are here."

"Never heard of anyone named Gavin before in my life."

"You haven't seen him here?" asked Lance.

Cora shook her head no. "You, Lance, are the first human I have ever seen here who was not a Myst."

Lance rubbed his hand over his head, "Interesting. Gavin is my spirit guide. He told me I was chosen to be one of God's Liberators, just as he was. So I just assumed you were a Liberator also because you are here."

"God's Liberator," whispered Cora more to herself than Lance. "Who are these Liberators?" asked Cora.

"Good question. All Gavin has ever mentioned is that I can control this world and the expectation is to 'end the pain that the Myst had started so long ago,' as Gavin put it," said Lance.

Cora squatted in the sand and sifted her hand through the grains and thought for a moment. She glanced back up at Lance and watched him as he looked around.

"So your physical body is asleep right now?" Cora asked.

"About that. I'm not sure."

Cora stood back up. “What do you mean?”

Lance looked at her, “The last thing I remember was leaving my apartment because one of those Myst creatures that I thought was my girlfriend attacked me. Somehow I fought back and killed the thing.” He paused and looked at the ground. “And in the process I think I killed my girlfriend also.”

Cora put her hand on his shoulder, “Do you mean it attacked you in the physical world? While you were awake? Not here?”

“Yes. Gavin warned me that the Myst were becoming bolder in order to kill me. He warned that they might drop the veil of secrecy to stop me from killing them.”

Cora shook her head. “It doesn’t make sense.”

“What doesn’t?”

“From what I know—and I don’t know how I know—but only a soul-lineage Myst can cross over the veil and enter our physical world,” explained Cora.

“What is a soul-lineage Myst?” asked Lance.

“Think of a soul-lineage Myst as a spider at the center of its web. Each knot of the web is a minor Myst that is attached to the soul-lineage Myst by the soul thread of the humans they host. If the soul-lineage Myst dies, the web dies, the minor Mysts die, and all of the human souls are released,” explained Cora.

“And those humans die,” stated Lance.

“Sadly, yes,” confirmed Cora.

“And their souls are free to begin again,” stated Lance.

“Reincarnation,” stated Cora.

XXXIV

Grace walked over to the hospital window of Lance's room and looked out at the night sky. She noticed next to the window two gargoyle statues perched as if protecting the room. She looked back at James, who was reading the attending doctor's notes. "James, did you see these gargoyles?" asked Grace.

James looked up from the notes and squinted at Grace because his glasses were perched on his head. "See what?"

"These gargoyle statues."

James walked over to the window and slid his glasses back over his eyes. He looked at the gray stone gargoyles. "No, I didn't see them. Interesting; usually they would be located on the roof to repel water," he said, puzzled. As he spoke he watched as one of the wing tips of the gargoyle fell off and crashed to the street below.

At that moment Grace and James both heard screams coming from the nurses' station. James raced out of Lance's hospital room and down the hall, with Grace following. James pushed through the crowd of doctors and nurses and found a young nurse dead on the floor with her eyes burnt black.

James's cell phone vibrated with a text message. He read the text message to himself, but loud enough for Grace to hear him. "Alpha and Beta Teams are dead! Eyes burnt black!—Mark."

Grace touched his arm, "What does that mean?"

"We had two teams of dogs with narcolepsy to test the effectiveness of new drugs."

Grace turned and looked down the hallway at Lance's room. "What about Lance?"

James started running down the hallway before Grace. He used the doorframe to help guide him into the hospital room. As Grace entered the room, she thought she saw the broken-winged gargoyle staring into the hospital room through the window.

Grace almost ran into James as she entered the room. They both watched as Lance jerked back in the bed and three long, bloody cuts appeared on his chest and stomach.

XXXV

Cora looked up and saw three vultures circle over their heads. One vulture swooped down out of the sky, targeting Lance. Before Cora could warn him, the vulture skimmed the top of his head. Lance ducked low enough to feel only the wing strike his head.

After the vulture flew past Lance it landed in the mixture of desert sand and golden grass behind him. Cora looked up in the sky for the other two vultures, but they were gone.

From behind Cora heard, "Leave now and we shall spare your life."

Cora turned and saw two Mysts standing behind her. Both silver aliens had golden eyes staring back at Cora. Cora looked back at Lance and saw the third Myst. She knelt to the ground and whispered, "Grumly, Bozz, come to me."

Lance watched as two sets of muscular hands broke through the mixture of desert soil and golden grass to pull their stone-covered bodies to the surface of the ground next to Cora. The two gargoyles unfolded and stretched their wings behind them as a way to announce their presence.

Cora calmly whispered, "Attack." The two gargoyles leapt from the ground and extended their wings in front of them. The points of their sharp wings glittered in the violet haze.

Lance raced over to Cora's side and unsheathed his two swords. "Nice pets," he commented.

Cora tried to suppress a smile as she unsheathed her two daggers. "Thanks."

The gargoyle named Grumly missed the Myst by inches when the Myst spun to strike a blow on the other gargoyle named Bozz on the wingtip with its claws. Bozz rolled in the golden grass and slowly got to his feet and brushed the dirt off of his severed wing tip. Grumly kicked the Myst in the back of the knees, bringing it to the ground. Bozz rejoined the fight by bounding across the ground to land on top of the Myst's chest. The gargoyle grabbed the silver alien's throat with his claws and ripped out half of the creature's neck. He raised the bloody mass of tissue in the air and growled in victory as the Myst's body went limp and a burst of white mist exploded into thousands of tendrils of vapor that rose up into the purple sky. Then the Myst's body disappeared.

In the purple sky Lance and Cora heard, "Their souls are free to begin again."

XXXVI

The air in Lance's lungs violently left his body as he hit the ground. With the loss of his breath, he also lost the grip on his two swords. The Myst jumped in the air in an effort to crush Lance under its clawed hands. At the last minute, Lance forced himself to roll to the side and miss the Myst's claws as they impaled the ground. Lance struggled quickly to his feet and checked the three cuts on his chest. The blood dripped down his stomach.

***

Cora waited for the third Myst to attack her. The creature lunged at her, crossing its clawed arms in front of its chest. Cora ducked and buried both daggers into the Myst's stomach. The alien howled in pain and brought both elbows down onto Cora's back. She collapsed to the ground under the crushing blow, feeling blood rushing from her back. As the Myst kicked her in the side, she saw bloody spikes extending from the creature's elbows. The Myst kicked Cora in the stomach, lifting her off the ground and sending her toward the edge of the nearby cliff. Grumly and Bozz slowly approached the fight and stalked the Myst from behind.

***

Lance waited for the Myst to rise to its feet to continue the fight—not out of honor, but in an attempt to catch his breath. Overhead, the sky shifted through several colors of red before remaining a constant purple with crimson red clouds. Cora knelt on the ground, struggling to rise to her feet. Lance watched as Grumly and Bozz moved closer to Cora in order to protect her from the enemy.

Unexpectedly, the Myst closest to Lance launched itself at him and struck him in the chest with both fists. Lance flew several feet from where he stood. He rolled to his feet and skidded to a halt. He braced himself for the next attack.

***

The sky shifted through a rainbow of colors again and Cora felt the wind blow across her face and body. Cora changed her strategy. She attacked the Myst that had just struck Lance. The flat part of her sword struck the creature in the back of the head and crumpled it to the ground. It quickly rolled to its feet and fled from the fight. Spinning her sword over her head, she struck the second Myst in the shoulder. The Myst spun around, kicking Cora in the legs, bringing her to the ground again. It quickly bent down and grabbed Cora by the throat. Lifting her off the ground, the Myst carried her to the edge of the cliff. The Myst dangled her struggling body over the edge of the cliff above the blackness. Cora held onto its forearm, struggling to find the ground. Bozz attacked the Myst by severing its forearm from the body. Cora fell over the cliff's edge. The Myst dropped to the ground, howling in pain.

***

Lance watched in horror as Cora fell from view. Being near the cliffs edge, he momentarily thought of jumping after her to catch her. Instead, the second gargoyle, Grumly, dove into the ground and disappeared into the soil only to emerge below Cora, catching her in the air. Bozz gnawed on the severed forearm of the Myst. Lance walked over and swung his sword across the Myst's neck. The Myst collapsed to the ground and thousands of white tendrils of vapor drifted off into the purple sky.

Lance stood on the edge of the bloody cliff and whispered, "Their souls are free to begin again."

***

Cora watched in horror as the last Myst, the one that had fled, materialized behind Lance and stabbed him in the back with its long, silver, clawed hand. Shock spread across Lance's face as he looked down at the protruding claws in his chest. Cora watched as he dropped to his knees and crumbled to the ground.

XXXVII

Grace and James watched as the doctors tried to revive Lance when his heart stopped beating. For several minutes they listened to the constant humming of the flatlined heart monitor. James reached out and touched the doctor's arm, indicating that it was enough. The doctor hesitated, stopped, and then announced the time of death. James walked over to the window and wrapped his arms around Grace to lead her out of the room as the nurse turned off the heart monitor.

Before Grace turned away from the window she noticed that the two gargoyle statues were gone. James led Grace outside of the hospital to get some fresh air. She leaned most of her body weight on him as she sobbed uncontrollably. James looked up into the night sky.

"Oh my god," he whispered.

Grace looked up at James and then the night sky, where he was pointing to the two full moons.

Book II

Luke was not even born when Neil Armstrong walked on the moon. But he did remember riding in his father's old Buick, pulling into a gas station when the radio announced that the space shuttle Challenger exploded. He remembered his father was on the verge of tears and Luke never really understood why. The nation mourned the loss of the shuttle and the astronauts. Then, as time passed, it was sadly forgotten. Even Luke had forgotten about the event until recently. Luke went about his life like every other seminormal American boy. He graduated from high school, went to college, found a wife, got her pregnant, and became a father.

Billy, his son, was three years old and was talking before Luke ever had at his age. His wife, Nadine, said it was normal for a three-year-old to talk, abnormal if he did not. Luke guessed he was abnormal. In either case, Billy was a joy and Luke loved spending as much time with him as his day allowed.

Nadine and Luke sat on the couch, watching the pre-show for the landing on the Earth's newly discovered moon. The thing that annoyed Luke the most about the pre-landing shows was the obsession by the media to pick a name for both of the Earth's moons. It seemed to Luke that society was more worried about naming the second moon than figuring out where it had come from or how it had stayed hidden for so long. Typical of society and the media, it was more important to apply names and labels to things they did not understand. At the same time, society and the media also realized that the original moon did not have a name either.

Luke knew that the reason the original moon did not have a name was that for hundreds of years it was thought that the Earth's moon was the only moon that existed in the night sky. In the seventeenth century, a scientist discovered other moons around other planets. Those moons were named so that humans could still distinguish Earth's own moon. Now, with the Earth having two moons, humans demanded names. Names were something society could grasp. Why the second moon appeared was something society feared.

With the appearance of the second moon, the International Space Agency, better known as the ISA, immediately made plans to land on it. For reasons unknown to Luke and the rest of the world, the newly designed space shuttles and lunar landers were given the designation of ISA Juddit. When the world media asked Why Juddit? the ISA simply stated that the crafts were being named after the man who discovered the second moon, a Lance Juddit. According to the media, Lance Juddit was a mystery.

The landing on the second moon by Juddit III was anticipated to be the most-watched event since the original moon landing in 1969. Luke had waited all week for the day so that the family could sit together and witness a piece of history in the making. He even went out and bought appetizers and Billy's favorite food to make it a special event. Luke wanted Billy to remember this moment for the rest of his life. Nadine thought Luke was making too much out of nothing. Luke ignored her little jabs all week long. He was doing this for Billy and maybe a little bit for himself. Sometimes he wondered if she meant the jabs. In either event, that night was important on so many levels.

From the living room couch Luke called out, "Billy, it's about to start."

Nadine and Luke heard the shuffle of little feet down the hallway into the living room. They both turned to look at their son as he stood in the entrance of the living room in his one-piece sleeper with booties. Nadine and Luke were both sitting on opposite ends of the couch. Billy usually liked to sit or lie in the middle so he could switch back and forth between leaning against his mother and father. This night he walked over to the couch and looked at his mother and then his father with a confused look on his face.

Luke asked him, "What's wrong, little guy?"

"There's no room for Jamie," he said.

His mother asked, "Who's Jamie, dear?"

Billy turned and waved his arm behind him toward the entrance of the living room as if he was going to introduce someone. No one stood in the entranceway.

"He's my friend," he said.

Nadine and Luke looked out in the hallway, half-expecting someone to step around the corner to show himself. But they both knew there was no one else in the house.

Luke put his hand on Billy's little shoulder and asked, "Who is Jamie?"

"My friend."

Luke could not see Jamie, and he knew that Nadine could not see him either. But Luke got up off of the couch and sat on the floor with his back against the couch. He grabbed both of Billy's hands and looked at him and smiled.

"You and Jamie can have my seat," Luke said.

"Thanks, Dad," Billy said.

Billy climbed over Luke to sit on the couch behind him. He sat with his back against the couch and his short little legs fluttered, trying to reach the end of the cushion.

Billy patted the last seat on the couch and said, "Come here, Jamie."

Luke had always been accused of having a vivid imagination, but if he had to swear to an unnamed god, he swore that he felt something step over his legs to sit next to Billy. Luke turned and looked back at Billy and the empty space on the couch. He could not see anything, but he felt something sitting next to Billy for the rest of the night as they watched Juddit III land on the second moon.

Billy fell asleep before Juddit III made its initial touchdown on the surface of the second moon. Nadine waited until the astronaut secured the newly formed Global Alliance flag onto the surface of the second moon and then went off to bed. When Nadine relinquished her seat from the couch, Billy's little body crashed to the cushions without waking him. Luke continued to watch all of the news channels late into the night as Billy slept on the couch.

Luke went to bed when the news channels began to recycle the videos of the second moon landing. He carried Billy to his bed and covered him in his blankets. He sat on the edge of the bed in the dark and watched his son for a few minutes before getting up to leave. As he moved to rise off the bed, Billy reached out and grabbed his hand.

"Daddy?"

Luke sat back down on the bed. "Yeah?"

"Is Jamie in the room?" he asked.

Luke found himself actually looking around the room for Jamie. He saw nothing, but still had that nagging feeling that something was there.

"Sure he is," Luke said.

"Where?" Billy asked.

"Um," Luke stammered, "in the doorway." He leaned back to let Billy look at the entrance.

Billy sat up in bed and looked at the open door. He smiled and lay back down.

"I'm glad," Billy said.

"Why?"

"So the monsters under the bed won't get me," said Billy as he rolled over onto his side.

Luke rubbed his back and thought about the monsters that lived under his bed when he was a child.

Curious, Luke asked, "Have you seen these monsters?"

Billy turned and looked at his father. "Yeah, but Jamie scares them off for me."

Billy closed his eyes to sleep. Luke did not push the subject. He kissed his son on the head and left the room. As he walked out, he hoped that Jamie was sitting in the corner waiting to protect his son from any demons he could not see.

Nadine was already asleep by the time Luke climbed into bed. He curled up behind her and closed his eyes.

***

Luke awoke with the sunlight in his eyes and was the last one to get up that morning. He went to bathroom and peed. He splashed water on his face. In the mirror he noticed a purple bruise on his right shoulder.

"What the hell?" he said.

Luke flexed his shoulder and rotated it over his head and the pain shot throughout his arm. He pulled a shirt over his chest and flinched when he had to put his bad arm through the shirtsleeve. He went down to the kitchen, where Nadine and Billy were already eating breakfast. Nadine gave Luke a quick hug and kiss good morning before she handed him an empty mug. Luke walked over to the table and rustled Billy's hair. He gave his son a kiss on the top of the head and mumbled, "Good morning."

Billy looked up at his dad and said good morning back with a mouth full of cereal and milk.

Luke walked over to the counter to fill his mug with coffee and asked, "Nadine, did I have any bad dreams last night?"

"No, I don't think so," she said. "Why?"

Luke poured his coffee. "My shoulder is sore. I thought maybe I was jerking in my sleep last night or something."

Nadine sat at the table and sipped at her coffee while she read the newspaper. "I don't know, dear."

Billy said with a mouth full of cereal, "It was the monster."

Nadine and Luke looked at Billy and asked together, "What?"

Billy looked back at the television and took another bite of cereal. His mother touched his shoulder.

Nadine asked, "What did you say?"

Billy looked at his mother. "The monster, under my bed."

Nadine looked at Luke to help her understand. Luke asked, "Do you mean the monster that Jamie is supposed to protect you from?"

"Yes."

Billy finished his cereal and put the dirty bowl in the kitchen sink and left the kitchen for the living room. Nadine sat staring at Luke, who suddenly forgot how to add sugar to his coffee.

"What is this about Jamie and a monster under his bed?" Nadine asked in an accusing tone.

Luke remembered how many sugars he needed in his coffee and added one extra because he could tell it was going to be one of those conversations, "Last night, when I put him to bed, I asked who Jamie was and why he was here. Billy says that Jamie is a friend of his that protects him from the monsters under his bed."

"Oh," said Nadine.

"Maybe he thinks the monster came after me last night, since Jamie was protecting him."

"And you encouraged this?" asked Nadine in a tone that Luke did not find attractive.

"I didn't do anything. I simply asked and he told me," defended Luke.

"But you had the opportunity to tell him that Jamie and monsters do not exist," stated Nadine.

Luke hesitated and added two extra scoops of powdered cream to his coffee. "Maybe to you they don't exist, but to Billy they do."

Nadine laughed in a harsh tone that was condescending and laced with ridicule. "Like I said, you encouraged it by not dispelling it," and then she took a sip of coffee. "I'll talk to him."

Defensively, Luke said, "No, it's normal for kids to have imaginary friends. Didn't you have one?" he asked.

"No," Nadine said sharply. "But I am sure you did."

Luke thought about it as he took a drink of his coffee that was too sweet and creamy. "I think I had an imaginary friend." He paused. "But I know there were monsters under my bed, in my closet, in the basement. They were always chasing me."

Nadine stood and tried to smile at him and said, "But, dear, you aren't normal," and walked out of the room.

As she left, Luke spoke up, "Babe, remember half of Billy comes from me." And smiled at his witty comeback.

Shooting him down, Nadine casually commented, "That's exactly what I'm afraid of."

***

Billy sat cross-legged on the floor in the living room watching television. Luke walked past the room and grinned when he saw Billy laughing at the television. He paused and took two steps backward to look into the room again because he noticed something that struck him as odd. Two human-shaped shadows stretched across the living room floor. The sun's rays from the front windows cast one shadow of Billy sitting cross-legged and a second shadow of a person lying on his stomach leaning on his elbows. Luke stepped into the room and both heads of the shadows turned to look at him. Billy smiled and turned back to the television. But the other shadow head continued to look at him. Luke felt the hairs on the back of his neck stand on end, and he slowly stepped out of the room.

As Luke removed himself from the room he heard Billy say, "Do you want some milk and cookies?" There was no response and then Luke heard Billy say, "Okay."

Luke watched as Billy walked out of the living room and into the kitchen. He overheard Billy ask his mother for some milk and cookies. Luke peeked his head around the corner into the living room and saw that both shadows were gone.

Luke overheard Billy say, "But I need a second glass of milk and cookies for Jamie."

"Okay, but you make sure he drinks all of his milk," Nadine said.

Billy walked past Luke carrying two small glasses of milk and placed them on the floor. He ran back into the kitchen to get the two plates of cookies. He sat on the floor and dipped a cookie into the milk and took a bite.

As Luke walked up the stairs to his home office he heard Billy ask, "I know, my mom is the best, isn't she?"

***

Channel 9 Breaking News!

The crew of Juddit III has discovered a group of freestanding structures during their initial ground survey of the currently unnamed second moon. The crew is currently preparing a reconnaissance mission to determine the origin of these structures.

***

A few hours later, when Billy was taking his afternoon nap, Nadine came into Luke's office.

She sat on his lap and kissed him on the temple, "Are you busy?"

"Not really. I need a break anyway," Luke said as he rested his head against her shoulder. "Is Billy sleeping?"

Nadine rubbed Luke's back, "Yeah, he laid down about thirty minutes ago."

"Is Jamie with him?" Luke asked.

Nadine laughed. "I don't know, he didn't say." She paused. "You know, I think Billy is going through another growth spurt."

"Why do you say that?" Luke asked.

"He finished both servings of milk and cookies I gave him this morning," said Nadine.

Luke looked at Nadine. "Are you sure Jamie didn't eat one of those portions?"

Nadine smiled and kissed Luke on the temple again. With her lips pressed against his temple she quietly mumbled, "Stop encouraging him." She pushed off of his lap and walked out of the office.

***

When dinner was finished and the dishes were cleaned up, Luke changed into a pair of shorts to go for a jog. He kissed Nadine on the shoulder and told her he would return within the hour. Billy was consumed by a pile of building blocks as he tried to build a fortress for his action figures and never noticed when Luke left. Luke walked briskly to the track behind his house to get the blood moving in his legs before he started his run.

As Luke walked over to the track he looked up at the night sky and saw that a few scattered clouds drifted in front of the two moons that had started their ascent across the sky. The one thing he noticed that he did not like about the second moon was that the additional reflected light of the second moon drowned out the nearby stars. Then again it could be the stadium lights of the high school softball team practicing or the fact that he lived in the city. He made a mental note to find an excuse to take Billy out into the country at night so he could see if there were fewer stars visible in the night sky.

Luke enjoyed jogging at night because there were fewer people on the track and it was much quieter for him to think. He figured that two miles this evening would be enough to stretch his legs and calm his nerves. He did not know why he felt jittery. Something was making him anxious. Maybe it was all that talk about Jamie or that he saw two shadows earlier that day when there was supposed to be only one. Or maybe it was his relationship with Nadine. He often wondered if it was him, but something was not right. Sometimes he felt that Billy was the only thing that kept them together. He shook his head. That was not a nice thought. It was not supposed to be like that.

Luke took a deep breath and pushed off of his left foot and started his jog. After a few strides he started to think more about Billy and Jamie. If he was honest with himself, he really was not upset that Billy saw or had an imaginary friend. He had seen imaginary friends his entire life. He still saw things. That was one of the reasons why he liked to jog at night. At night he saw the most things. Maybe that is what was bothering him this evening. He did see things, but Nadine never believed him. He had tried to tell her, to explain to her what he saw. But she always ridiculed him, so he stopped.

Luke knew that for most people jogging around a track multiple times can be boring. But for Luke jogging around the track was almost a form of meditation: a simple labyrinth that transcended his mind to a higher spiritual plane. As he jogged he looked up at the night sky and watched the stars and moons as they stood guard over his world. Occasionally he would see movement in the corner of his eyes, but it was usually during the fourth or fifth lap of his jog that he saw the man in black standing at the painted starting line of the track.

Luke knew the man in black was not real in the sense that he was a breathing human being of this world or this dimension. To Luke, the man in black was a part of his imagination—like Jamie, but he never gave the man in black a name. When he was younger he was scared of the man in black. Now that he was older he was apprehensive, but not scared. He had come to realize that the man in black was not there to hurt him. But still at times it could be a little unnerving to have a man in black watch you.

Oftentimes when Luke jogged at night he felt the man in black running behind him. When he felt brave he would extend his arm behind him as if he were waiting to receive a baton during a relay. What Luke was really doing was hoping to feel the man in black. Luke hoped to grab hold of the cape that wrapped around the man in black, or simply feel the man's touch against his own hand. Luke often wondered why he wanted to feel the touch of the man in black. Maybe if he could feel the man in black, his mind would accept that what he saw was real. But if the man in black was real, what would that do to his imagination?

When Luke was younger he often saw things at night and sometimes during the day. He quickly learned whom he could tell and whom he could not tell. Nadine fell in that category of whom he could not tell—which bothered him because he always assumed he could tell his wife everything and she would accept him for him.

However, that myth of spousal acceptance was quickly shattered the first time he told Nadine about the man in black. Now, with the appearance of the second moon, Luke regularly experienced strange creatures flying across the treetops that looked like bats the size of crows, dancing lights, voices, dragons, UFOs, and many other unexplained things. He wished he could share what he experienced with Nadine.

He was not the only person experiencing strange sightings after the second moon appeared. Luke started to overhear neighbors and patrons at the local coffee shop talk about strange happenings. One neighbor said his gargoyles came to life and ate all of the tomatoes in his garden. Another neighbor said the gnome statues in his front yard ate the roses, and the stone dog ran away. When Luke retold those stories to Nadine, she always dismissed them and said they were farfetched or untrue. Luke was too embarrassed to express his true feelings about those stories to Nadine for fear that she would make fun of him.

***

Luke got home in time to give Billy a sweaty kiss goodnight and then jumped in the shower. Nadine read Billy a story and tucked him in under the covers. As she walked out of the room and pulled the door closed, Billy asked, "Mom, can you leave the door open?"

Nadine pushed the door back open. "Sure honey."

"Thanks, Mom."

Nadine walked into the bedroom wearing a robe over a pair of old sweatpants and a college T-shirt that was approximately three sizes too big for her. She hung the robe on the freestanding coat rack that stood in the corner of the room. Luke joined Nadine in bed and they talked about nothing as they lay next to each other. Luke wanted to reach out and touch her leg but he did not. He just wanted to be close to her. As a kid he remembered always seeing his parents cuddle or watch them lie in bed and reminisce about their lives together. He and Nadine never did anything of the sort when they lay in bed together. He chuckled to himself and thought, Hell, we don't even make love.

"What's so funny?" asked Nadine.

"Uh, what?" asked Luke as her voice broke into his thoughts.

"Why did you chuckle?" asked Nadine.

In the dark he could feel that her head was turned facing him and waiting for an answer. "I was just thinking that we never make love anymore." The minute the words came out of his mouth, he knew he should have said something different. He should have lied.

Without a word, Nadine rolled over on her side facing away from Luke and went to sleep.

***

Nadine heard Billy screaming in his sleep. She hurried to his side to calm him down. Luke vaguely remembered feeling Nadine get out of bed. He lay there staring at the ceiling, trying to get his bearings, when he felt two strong hands grab his ankles and pull him out of bed. He found himself hanging upside down, with his arms outstretched and his hands almost touching the floor. Luke looked at the ground and saw two large, black, hairy feet under his head. Before he was able to look up at the ceiling, he heard Nadine calling from Billy's room.

"Luke, Luke can you get Billy a glass of water please?" she yelled from their son's room.

For a moment Luke felt a surge of irritation rush through his body as he wondered why she could not get the glass of water. Then he remembered that even if he wanted to get the glass of water, he couldn't because he was several feet off the floor, held upside down by some creature with hairy feet that had pulled him out of bed. The thing holding Luke tossed him against the closet doors. Luke hit the doors sideways and crashed to the floor hard.

Luke heard Nadine again. "Luke!" she said with a hint of irritation in her voice as she walked down the hallway. Luke watched as the creature dove its long, thick body underneath the bed as Nadine walked into the bedroom.

"What the hell are you doing on the floor?" asked Nadine, with no effort to hide her irritation.

Luke looked at Nadine and scrambled toward the bed to look under it. As soon as he looked under the bed he saw a pair of yellow eyes peer out at him. He quickly pushed away from the bed and stood up. Still staring at the bed and trying to control his body from shaking apart, Luke mumbled, "I tripped."

"God, you are pathetic when you first wake," she said. "Do you think you can make it down the stairs to get your son a glass of water?"

Luke did not answer Nadine. He just left the room and walked down the stairs to get Billy a glass of water. As he descended the steps to the kitchen a fleeting thought ran through his head: Why can't that fucking creature attack you! He realized that was not nice and shook his head to try to dismiss the thought.

As Luke returned up the stairs to Billy's room, he knew that Nadine had gone back to bed. The tableside light in Billy's room was still on. His son was sitting up in bed when Luke walked in.

Luke asked, "Are you okay?"

Billy nodded his head yes and took the glass from his father's hands. Luke sat on the edge of the bed as Billy took a drink of the water. Billy slurped the excess water on his lips and handed the glass back to Luke. Billy then lay down and pulled the covers up to his neck. Luke kissed him on the forehead and whispered, "I love you." He then pushed off the bed to turn off the bedside light. Luke turned to walk out of the room. As he reached the door Billy asked, "Did you get hurt?"

"What?" asked Luke, trying to keep the surprise out of his voice.

"Did the monster hurt you?" Billy asked a second time.

Luke walked back to Billy's bed and sat down. He brushed the hair from his son's forehead. "No," he said softly.

Luke could feel Billy smile in the dark. "Good, Jamie was protecting me. Sorry he couldn't come protect you."

Luke took in a deep breath and continued to run his fingers through his son's hair. "Jamie is a good friend."

"Goodnight, Dad."

Luke sat for a moment longer and stared at his son in the dark. He brushed his son's cheek with the back of his fingers and got up to leave the room. Luke walked across the hall to his and Nadine's bedroom and said a quick prayer that she would be asleep.

Unfortunately, his prayer was not answered because when he walked in the room Nadine asked, "Is he asleep?"

"Yeah," Luke said as he stared at the dark space under the bed from the doorway. As he stood in the doorway he contemplated jumping from the threshold to the bed. He shook his head. He knew Nadine would flip her shit on him for pulling a stunt like that. But the thought of walking and standing next to his bed so the creature under the bed could grab his legs flipped him out.

Nadine's voice broke him out of his thoughts when he heard her ask, "What are you doing?"

Luke contemplated telling her the truth. I'm trying to figure out if I am more scared of you or the creature under the bed. Instead he decided that would go over about as good as when he chuckled because they never made love anymore. He took a deep breath, found what little courage he had, cursed society for the demands it put on men, and slowly walked to his side of the bed. Standing beside the bed he wiggled his toes and almost wished the creature would reach out and grab his ankles so he could prove to Nadine that what he saw and experienced was real. Nothing happened.

"Luke, will you please get in bed so I can go to sleep. I have to get up early tomorrow morning," complained Nadine.

Luke climbed into bed and pulled the covers over his body. He continued to play the scene over and over again in his head. For a moment he sat up in bed and grabbed his ankles, wondering if there were marks to prove that he was pulled out of bed. Nadine tossed on her side of the bed and mumbled something. Luke lay back down and stared at the ceiling, wishing he could cuddle with someone until he fell asleep. Instead, he stared at the ceiling until the early morning rays of the sun crept around the corners of the blinds.

***

"Extraterrestrial" Structures Discovered on the Second Moon

Dustin Hollinsworth

dhollinsworth@jeffersonpost.com

The International Space Agency and the Global Alliance have both confirmed that the exploration team of Juddit III has discovered extraterrestrial structures on the surface of the second moon. At this time the exploration team is unable to determine the purpose of the structures. After a preliminary sweep of the area, Captain Louis speculates the buildings are sleeping quarters. Even though the ISA and the Global Alliance have both confirmed the existence of these structures on the second moon, they are at odds on the next course of action. ISA has granted Captain Louis and his team the green light to gather more information and make contact if that is an option. The Global Alliance has adamantly stated precaution and the evacuation of Juddit III from the surface.

***

Nadine sat on the edge of the bed and kissed Luke on the forehead and waited for him to open his eyes. Luke stirred to pretend that he was just waking up because he did not want to talk with

Nadine that morning. She gently shook his shoulder and asked, "Did you break the closet door last night?"

Luke had to control his facial expression and eyes from betraying that he really had been awake since she got up to get in the shower to get ready for work. Instead he faked a sleepy, "Huh?"

Nadine asked again, "Last night when you tripped out of bed. Did you fall into the closet door? One of the wheels in the track is broken."

Luke rolled over in bed trying to distance himself from Nadine. "Actually, I was pulled out of bed by a really large monster and it threw me into the closet door when you went to go check on Billy."

Nadine sat quietly on the edge of the bed for a few seconds before saying anything. "It's one thing for Billy to say such things because he is a little boy." She paused. "But for you, it is a pathetic way to get attention. Keep it up and I'll demand that you get help." She stalked out of the room and down the stairs.

Luke opened his eyes. "Screw you," he said as she walked down the stairs. He half-hoped she heard him.

***

Later that afternoon when Billy was asleep in his room for his afternoon nap, Luke brought the old baby monitor into his office. Earlier in the day he had dug it out of Billy's closet and hid it in his son's room. Now, he plugged the receiver in his office and turned on the volume. Luke adjusted the volume until he could hear Billy's soft, easy breathing as he slept. His breathing was slow and continuous. Luke sat at his desk, leaned back in his chair, and closed his eyes to listen. He thought about how from the first time they brought Billy home he would lie in bed and listen to his son breathe. It was a sound that always calmed his nerves and brought a smile to his face. Luke found himself drifting off to sleep when he heard Billy's voice coming from the baby monitor.

"Is there anything under there?" said Billy.

Luke's eyes shot open and he leaned forward in his chair to stare more intently at the baby monitor.

Billy continued, "Look in the closet. They hide in there also."

"There is nothing Billy, I scared them all away," said a new voice.

"What the hell?" asked Luke out loud. He reached out and grabbed the baby monitor with both hands. That had to be Billy using a pretend voice, thought Luke.

Billy spoke again, "They scare me, Jamie."

The voice answered, "Go to sleep. You need your rest. I promise to protect you."

"Who will protect my parents?" asked Billy.

"Your parents don't need protecting," answered the voice.

Luke heard Billy start to sniffle like he did when he began to cry. Luke wanted to race up to his son's room to comfort him. Instead he sat frozen in his chair listening to the conversation in bewilderment.

Billy sniffed again. "Yes, they do."

"Billy, I can't protect your parents if they don't believe," the voice said.

"Why?" asked Billy, still sniffling.

"Parents lose their ability to believe as they get older. Grown-ups believe they know all the answers and turn away from help that is willing to guide them," explained the voice. "Go to sleep, Billy, please."

Billy did not ask any more questions and the voice no longer talked. The only sounds coming from the monitor were Billy's breathing as he slept. Luke finally felt the strength in his legs and was able to stand up from his chair. He slowly walked up the stairs and down the hall to Billy's room. The door was open far enough to allow Luke to peek his head into the room to check on his boy. He saw Billy lying on his side, quietly sleeping. In the corner of his eye, Luke thought he saw another boy sitting in the foam cushion chair in the corner of the room. He turned to look at the foam chair and saw nothing.

He whispered, "I believe," then stepped out of the room.

***

The other boy in the corner uncrossed his arms from his chest and watched Billy's father turn and walk back down the hall.

***

Three Missing! Immediate Lift-Off for Juddit III!
Dustin Hollinsworth
dhollinsworth@jeffersonpost.com

The Global Alliance reports that Captain Louis and two other crew members from Juddit III have disappeared and are presumed dead. According to ISA, Captain Louis and his exploration team entered the found structures and communication immediately ceased with Houston. The remaining crew have reported no activity from the structures. By order of the ISA, the remaining crew of Juddit III were ordered for immediate take-off from the surface of the second moon. The Global Alliance has requested that Juddit III return to Earth immediately in case the disappearance of Captain Louis and his team results from an act of aggression. ISA states Juddit III will remain in orbit of the second moon until further notice.

***

That night Luke was not sure if he was unable or unwilling to tell Nadine what he heard or felt that afternoon in Billy's room. A part of him knew that if he told Nadine, she would just make fun of him, while another part of him felt that he had to protect Jamie and

Billy from Nadine. Luke had replayed Billy and Jamie's conversation in his head all day long. Maybe Jamie was right. Maybe adults do lose something as they get older—maybe the ability to see the unknown or simply the magic to believe when others do not. One thing that Luke did know was that it was harder to have an open mind and believe when no one supported you. Subconsciously, maybe that is why he never told Billy he was being silly believing in Jamie. Luke wanted Billy to know that at least one adult person believed in his world.

By the time Luke finished reading Billy his favorite story and let the dog out for the night, Nadine was already asleep in bed. She had fallen asleep with the bedside light on and the book she was reading resting on her chest. Before Luke turned off her light he went to his side of the bed and knelt down to peer under it. He half-expected to see a pair of yellow eyes staring back at him. Instead he just saw the usual junk that neither he nor Nadine needed, but refused to throw away for some odd reason.

Luke pushed up off the ground and walked to Nadine's side and removed the book from her chest and marked the page. Luke turned off the light and got down on his knees again to check under her side of the bed. He smiled to himself thinking that maybe the creature with the yellow eyes was a manifestation of Nadine's perpetual negative attitude toward everything concerning him. He was just about to look under the bed when he heard Nadine move. He looked up at Nadine and tried to find a hint of a smile on her face but only saw disdain.

"What are you doing?" she asked.

"Looking for monsters," Luke said with as much confidence as he could gather.

"You are unbelievable," Nadine said and rolled onto her back.

Luke grabbed the bed skirt and thought twice about looking under the bed. Instead he climbed into bed and lay on his side, facing away from Nadine. The silence in the room was thick. He could feel her watching him as he tried to fall asleep.

***

Billy awoke that night screaming. Luke jumped out of bed and ran into his son's bedroom in giant leaps. Billy sat in the corner of his bed against the wall with the covers pulled up around his neck, screaming. Luke slid across the bed and wrapped Billy in his arms. With his one hand Luke pressed Billy's tear-stained face into his chest. Billy's sobs were uncontrollable, his voice inaudible. Luke continued to hold him tight against his body. He could feel Billy's tears soak through his shirt as his little body shook with fear. Luke slowly eased Billy to the edge of the bed to try to carry him out of the room.

Just as Luke's foot touched the floor Billy screamed out, "No!"

Luke brought his foot back up to the bed and frantically asked, "What's wrong?"

"They'll get you." Before Luke could ask who, Billy continued, "The monsters."

Luke grabbed the sides of his son's head and forced him to look in Luke's eyes. "I'm going to take you back to Mommy and Daddy's bed, where you will be safe."

Billy whispered, "Please no, Daddy," but Luke did not hear him. Instead Luke stepped onto the floor and pushed himself off the bed as Billy clung tighter to his body. As Luke walked across the room, Billy cried harder and squeezed against his daddy as hard as he could. When Luke crossed the threshold of Billy's door he quickly walked through the hallway to the master bedroom. Before Luke and Billy walked through the entrance to the master bedroom, the door slammed shut in Luke's face. The force of the door knocked him backward onto the hallway floor. Luke pressed off the floor to his knees, ready to yell at Nadine, assuming she was the one that slammed the door shut in his face. He held his tongue when the door opened and he saw two yellow eyes framed by a huge, black, hairy creature standing in the doorframe staring at him. Billy buried his head under his arms as he balled up on the floor. Luke tried to crawl backward to Billy's room but was frozen in place more out of shock than fear. The creature reached out and tried to grab at Luke but screamed in pain as its arm broke the threshold of the door. The creature quickly retracted its arm. Luke pulled away from the monster's grasp. The creature growled at him in hatred. Violently, the creature stumbled forward as if being pushed from behind. It was evident that the creature was caught off-guard by the shove and stumbled through the doorframe. The creature's foot stepped out in the hallway to catch its balance. The creature howled in pain as steam rose from the carpet of the hallway. It quickly pulled its leg back into the bedroom and hopped back to the bed to support itself. A teenage boy, Luke assumed was Jamie, tried to run out of the master bedroom into the hallway. But the creature grabbed his ankle and he fell to the ground halfway through the door. Jamie grabbed Billy's foot and held on. Billy screamed in surprise. He tried to pull his foot away. When he saw it was Jamie, he reached down and grabbed onto Jamie's hand with both of his. The creature gave a hard yank on Jamie's ankle and he and Billy both slid closer to the bedroom entrance. Luke grabbed Billy's outstretched arms and pulled as hard as he could to get his son back. Jamie lost his grip on Billy's foot and disappeared back into the bedroom.

Luke grabbed Billy and pulled him against the wall in the hallway. He held his head in both of hands. "Billy, listen to me. You have to stay here! The monster won't hurt you; they can't leave the bedrooms."

Billy nodded his head yes as the tears streamed down his cheeks. "But what about Jamie?" asked Billy.

Luke kissed his son on the forehead. "I got him," he said and dove into the bedroom head first before he realized what he was doing. Luke rolled and jumped to his feet in the middle of the room and looked around.

Nadine was asleep in bed.

"You've got to be kidding me," said Luke.

Jamie was nowhere to be seen.

The creature was hiding.

A thought flew through Luke's head. Maybe the creature was not hiding. He walked over to the bed to get a closer look at Nadine. She appeared to be sleeping.

The creature grabbed the top of Luke's head and threw him into the wall adjacent to the bed. Pain shot through his entire body. As he slid down the wall, he wondered if the pain was from hitting the wall or realizing that Nadine was not the monster. When he hit the ground he saw Jamie jump off of the dresser and onto the creature's back. He wrapped both arms around the creature's neck. The creature reached behind its head trying to grab Jamie.

Jamie yelled out to Luke, "Closet."

Luke ran across the bedroom and threw all of his body weight against the creature, knocking it several feet toward the closet. The monster grabbed Luke's right hip and tossed him aside as if he was a doll. Luke hit the ground and rolled into the wall. He did not hesitate. He jumped off the ground and rushed the monster again. This time when he hit the creature and clung to its greasy fur, it stumbled toward the closet. Jamie continued to choke the creature as Luke continued to push it toward the open closet door. The creature stumbled again and caught the edge of the closet before it fell into the darkness of clothes.

Jamie let go of the creature's neck and dropped to the floor. Luke was still holding onto the creature's waist when Jamie gave the thing a running push that toppled it over the edge of the closet door. As soon as the creature crossed the threshold, the closet changed from hanging clothes and shoes to a giant black pit. Luke fell into the black hole along with the creature.

Jamie grabbed his foot and held onto him as Luke watched the creature disappear into the darkness. Jamie pulled Luke out of the closet and laid him on the bedroom floor. He collapsed next to Luke, breathing hard. Without looking at Jamie, Luke asked, "What are you?"

Jamie smiled at the ceiling. "Billy's imaginary friend."

"No shit," Luke said, "but what are you? I can see you, hear you, and feel you, but you look almost transparent."

"Billy created me from his mind to protect him," answered Jamie.

"Protect him from that monster?" Luke asked.

"Yes, those monsters that your fears created," said Jamie as he stood up to brush the thing's greasy fur off of him.

"What?" Luke asked as he got up with him. "My fears?"

Jamie turned and looked up at Luke. "Your fears and Nadine's fears. Both of you pass your fears on to your offspring through your DNA. It's natural."

"Natural? Sounds unhealthy and unfair," protested Luke.

Jamie shrugged his shoulders and turned toward the bedroom door to check on Billy. Luke saw his son sitting quietly in the hallway next to the black burn mark of a paw on the carpet.

Jamie turned toward Luke and put his hand on his shoulder. "Don't worry. You've already helped him."

"How?" asked Luke.

Jamie turned and looked at Billy. "You believe in his imaginary friend." He paused and looked back to Luke. "You see me."

Luke smiled and stepped out into the hallway. He outstretched his arms and Billy sprang from the floor with excitement and relief. Luke picked him up and gave him a tight squeeze.

"Is it gone?" Billy asked his father.

Jamie answered, "Forever."

Billy looked down at Jamie and then his father in surprise. "You can see Jamie?"

Luke laid his son down in his bed and pulled the covers up over his shoulders. "Yes, I can see your friend Jamie."

Billy leaned toward his dad and kissed him and whispered, "I love you."

"I love you too," whispered Luke.

***

Jamie and Luke watched Billy until he drifted off to sleep. Luke walked to the bedroom door and Jamie sat in the inflatable chair in the corner. Luke looked at his son and then Jamie.

Jamie said, "Don't worry. I'll watch over him."

"I know," said Luke. "Good night." He pulled the door shut but left it open a crack just in case his son or Jamie called out for him.

***

Channel 9 Breaking News!
Juddit III presumed destroyed!

Book III

The three most powerful words in the English language are,
"I need you."
—Unknown

I

How many days and nights have I
Failed to look into your eyes?
How many months since we
Last touched?
How many years since we
Last spoke?
Too many to count, too many
To remember.

I reach for you, but I can
Not hold you.
I call out your name, but I
Do not hear you.
I gaze at you, but I
See nothing.
You only live in my dreams, where
You are alive.

Your eyes are as a calm storm,
Asking to be closer.
Your skin is soft, and desires to
Be touched.
Your hands reach out, wanting
To be held.
Willing, I come to you,
With love in my heart.

I look into your eyes,

And see compassion.
I touch your skin,
And you shiver.
I grasp your hands,
And it begins.

We, together become one,
With eternity.
Our love grows stronger,
By day.
Our passion,
By night.
Together we are strong,
Together we fall.

You slip your hands through mine,
And your eyes look away.
You turn to walk,
I reach for you, nothing.
You disappear into the darkness,
Tears flood my eyes.
I am alone, and the night
Consumes my fears.

Your happiness brought me light,
For a moment.
Only memories and wants
Exist in my heart.
Dreams and nightmares will pass,
Until our eyes meet again.
Until then, your love is the only
One I cherish.

***

The night the second moon appeared in the night sky, Jack Cooper read the lines of poetry he had written years before. He was never one to write, let alone something that halfway resembled a poem. He sat back in his chair and closed his eyes to remember the visions of his dream.

***

It was dark and his soul was free-floating in open space. The blackness lacked any sense of smell or sound. His soul's vision saw a faint white light spinning in the blackness. He willed himself to be near the light and felt his soul drift toward the whiteness. As he got closer to the light, the light took the shape of a beautiful woman. He was captive to the magnificent beauty as he moved closer. She turned and met his eyes, and Jack felt pure happiness spread throughout his soul. For the first time in his life he felt complete.

He felt whole.

Their hands clasped.

Their eyes locked.

Their souls entwined.

The meaning of happiness was embodied in this beautiful woman.

He instantly understood what love meant.

At that moment he knew soulmates were real.

At that same moment her hands slipped from his grasp.

Her eyes looked away.

Her soul parted from his.

And he watched as the beautiful light of the soul floated away from him into the darkness.

***

Jack opened his eyes and took a deep breath and placed the words he wrote in a desk drawer. He stood and walked to the kitchen and poured himself a glass of water. He moved to the front window of the living room. He looked across the street and watched one of his neighbors stumble from his car to their front door in a drunken haze.

He looked up at the night sky and at the two moons that hung toward the western horizon. He finished his glass of water in a single gulp and turned to go back to bed. He crossed the living room to his bed to lie down.

II

Sydney Jagger took a puff of her cigarette and crossed her arms over her chest. She held the smoke in her lungs for a few seconds and then blew it from her lips. She looked up at the twin-moon night and thought about the night the second moon appeared. That was the night she met her soulmate.

***

She was spinning in the darkness, alone and afraid. She felt hands reach out and clasp her shoulders with strength and tenderness. They spun her around. She saw the eyes of her soulmate.

She saw the beauty of his heart.

She felt the depth of his soul.

She embraced his intense passion.

She clasped his hands.

Embraced his love.

She let her soul become one with him.

Then her mind ripped her away from him.

Reality pulled her hands from his.

She turned her eyes away from him.

Her soul tore from his.

The darkness never looked so black when she forced herself to turn away.

***

She knew why she had turned away. She had another man. He filled her needs. She knew he was not the soul that had brushed against hers so many nights before. She had settled.

Now, all these years later, she regretted settling. She regretted pulling and turning away. She often wondered what would have happened if she had held onto her soulmate. Now staring up at the twin moons was her only reminder that she had touched her soulmate once in her life.

She flicked her cigarette butt into the neighbor's yard and went back into the house. She climbed into bed alone and drifted off to a restless night's sleep.

III

Kenny stood in the front yard of his house and watched as the light clicked off in the master bedroom. He knew Sydney would not ask him where he had been if he walked in before she went to bed. He just did not want to deal with her. She had become so cold and distant to him. He assumed there was a reason. But he really did not care.

He looked down at the tattoo on the palm of his hand. It was an equilateral triangle with a line through two sides. He clenched his fist and then opened it again. That tattoo was the sign of the Seekers. The Seekers of the Liberators. He noticed the symbol on his friend's calf one day at the gym. He asked him about it because it was the same symbol he had seen in his dreams for most of his life. His friend, Cory, said he belonged to a secret organization. Kind of like a fraternity, but larger, more important. On an impulse, Kenny asked if he could attend one of the meetings. His friend agreed without hesitation.

Now, months later, he was a full-fledged member, by evidence of the tattoo. He knew Sydney would never ask him about the tattoo. He was already covered with others. She would just ignore it like she had the others. He had no desire to tell her about the Seekers. Or their purpose. Kenny himself was still trying to figure out the purpose of the group. Even becoming a member did not reveal all the secrets of the organization. From what he gathered, the Seekers of the Liberators were as old as the Freemasons. And apparently just as secretive. Everything was on a need-to-know basis. The one thing the leader of their group stressed was there would come a time they would be contacted to perform a great service for their organization. That one purpose resonated with Kenny. If someone asked him why, he did not think he could answer that question. However, he knew in his heart that when the time came, he would not hesitate to perform the service for the greater good of the Seekers of the Liberators.

IV

Jack walked the edge of the labyrinth and ignited each of the nine torches that ringed the perimeter. He stood at the beginning of the labyrinth and took a deep breath through his nose and slowly exhaled. He closed his eyes and whispered a prayer. "Lord, thank you for this evening. Thank you for providing me with the gift and guidance to create this labyrinth. Please continue to guide me down the path that you wish for me to follow."

He bowed slightly and took a tentative step onto the path of the labyrinth. "Please let her hear me tonight," whispered Jack as he took his second step. With each step through the labyrinth Jack thought about the one soul he had touched so many years before. He twisted and turned through each ring of the labyrinth. His mind never wavered or faltered from the intention in his heart to make contact with his soulmate again. With each step he could feel his soul vibrate as it ascended higher into the universe.

Jack reached the center of the labyrinth and kneeled. With his eyes closed and palms on his knees he let his body settle. He started the first of twelve breaths. With each breath he felt his soul ascend higher into the universe. With each breath his soul-eyes could see white threads hanging from the sky. On his twelfth breath he pushed off the ground and willed his soul body to fly through the white threads in search of the one soul he sought.

In the physical world Jack continued to focus on his breathing. He fought to control the excitement that coursed through his body. The night after the dream when he felt his soulmate he was convinced there was a way to reach her again. He had forsaken his education and all other relationships to try to find a way to touch her soul again. He spent years researching the concept of soul travel, or astral travel, as it is known in some circles. From what he learned, he constructed the labyrinth as a tool for his soul to transcend his body into the universe.

The first time Jack's soul lifted from his physical body he was beyond excited. He was elated. His soul lifted high into the night sky. He could see anywhere and everywhere. But his physical body's excitement got the better of him and his soul was pulled back into his body like a recoiled spring. The return was a shock to his system. He was not sure, but he thought he might have passed out for two days because of that experience.

He continued to practice. Over time Jack learned that his soul and body were connected by what he called a soul thread. He assumed this was a safety measure by God so his soul would always find a way back to his body. Jack also deduced that everyone on the planet had a soul thread, and he could see them. The one thing that he found curious about the soul threads was their different colors. Some were white and others were silver, yellow, red, and even black.

He thought one day he would explore the different colors. But for now his focus was to find the soul thread to his soulmate.

One night while Jack was practicing and drifting through the soul threads he thought of his mom. He felt his soul being tugged in a different direction than he was facing. His soul flew through the air and then abruptly stopped in front of a single soul thread. He followed it down to the ground and found his mother on the other end. She was sitting in the living room of his childhood home reading a book. He gasped and she looked up like she had heard him. He reached out and touched her on the shoulder and she brushed her arm as if she were swatting a fly. Jack's excitement got the better of him and he slung-shot back to his body. This time he thought he was only passed out for a day. Maybe a little longer.

This night Jack would pace himself. When his soul ascended into the clouds he would think of the soul in his dream. He hoped that would be enough to bring him to his soulmate's thread. He told himself he would just watch her. Nothing more. When Jack's soul reached the clouds, he thought of the dream. He thought of his soulmate and instantly he felt his soul sail through the night sky. He watched as buildings and mountains passed under him. He watched as soul threads parted ways for him to pass. He watched as the great ocean appeared on the horizon. Then he stopped. His soul was floating in front of one lone soul thread.

Jack's soul did not hesitate; it descended quickly. It passed through the roof of the house and through the top floor into a living room. Sitting on the couch was the soul of his mate. He knew without a doubt it was her. Even years later her soul glowed with the same white intensity it had when they floated in the darkness together. In all of his excitement to find her, Jack lost control of himself and whispered to her.

V

"I love you," said a voice.

Sydney sat up from the couch and looked at her husband, leaning against the arm of his recliner and softly snoring. Her glimmer of hope faded as she realized that she must be hearing things. She sighed and ran her fingers through her long hair. She used the remote control to turn off the television. After placing the remote control on the end table she pulled a blanket over Kenny's medium-size frame. She kissed him in a motherly fashion on the head and turned off the light as she left the living room.

Sydney stood a proud five feet and eleven inches tall. It took her years to learn the confidence to stand straight, with her head held high. As she crossed through the house she remembered how awkward she felt in high school, being the tallest girl in the class. Her father, who she believed towered over her, always told her that in time she would learn to love her height and everything about herself. She smiled at the thought of her father.

Sydney thought of her father often, but he never filled the void like she needed. Her father worked too much. He was a professor and a researcher. When her mother died, her father sank further into his research. She had a feeling that if it were not for her, her father would have joined her mother. She would never ask her dad, but it's what she felt in her heart.

Sydney thought of Kenny and knew in her heart that he did not fill the void within her. Sydney would agree with her friends that Kenny took care of her basic needs but he did not understand her. When she tried to explain what she wanted in a soulmate, everyone looked at her in a funny way, as if they had no idea what she was talking about or felt. She often wondered how so many people could be blind to the possibility of feeling so complete. She wondered if they just could not feel the possibility or if the passion had burned out of the universe long before? It made her sad to think that true love might be dying in the world.

"What happened to Cupid?" she mumbled out loud. Sydney found herself in the bedroom staring out the window at the two moons and the clouds passing by them. She wrapped her arms around her body and held herself tight. The thought of the dream with her soulmate passed through her memory. She wished there was a way that she could find him in the physical world. If she did, what would she do? She could never leave Kenny. It would be unfair to him. Unfair to her family. She tilted her head a little farther back to prevent the tears from rolling down her cheeks. She wondered why she had to suffer for everyone else. Sydney looked back at the moons and wondered if her soulmate could see the same two moons she saw. She wondered if he was looking at them right now.

Sydney smiled.

He was. She knew. The thought warmed her.

Sydney turned from the window and lit a handful of candles around the room. She pulled back the covers of her bed and climbed under the sheets. She pulled the extra pillow to herself and hugged it tight.

Sydney watched the candlelight reflect on the ceiling as she let her mind drift away. With her eyes half-closed her thoughts took her to a stone tunnel lit by torches. She followed the tunnel, tracing both of her hands along the walls. She could feel the rough texture of the stone on her fingertips causing her sleeping fingers to flex.

Sydney followed the torches to a 180-degree turn in the tunnel. She turned the corner and saw a large room with a circular design carved on the floor. Around the room were nine burning torches. In the middle of the circular design knelt a man with his back to her.

Sydney heard the words again, "I love you." She knew they came from the man kneeling. Her vision faded and the stone room disappeared. She opened her eyes and saw the dim candlelight flicker against the ceiling.

VI

Jack whispered, “I love you.” He could not control himself, or maybe it was his soul that he could not control. In either event, the words escaped from him when he saw her. He was momentarily afraid that the connection would be broken and he would be slung-shot back to his body. Instead he felt her soul reach out to his. He had made contact and almost could not believe it. All of his hard work had paid off.

He rose from his kneeling position and retraced his steps out of the labyrinth and back to the beginning. He walked back through the stone tunnel past the dying embers of the torches. At the end of the tunnel was a stone ladder that led to a wooden hatch. Jack ascended the ladder and pushed the hatch open into his kitchen. He pulled his body through, closed the hatch, and finally covered it with a throw rug. In his two-room house he crossed through the kitchen to the living area and collapsed on the bed. He looked up through the skylight and saw that dawn was approaching. Jack crossed his arms behind his head and smiled. He had finally done it. He had finally made contact with his soulmate. His smile broadened at the thought of the passion he sensed from her soul.

VII

Sydney kept her eyes closed while still in bed and extended her arm to feel for Kenny. When she did not feel him she opened her eyes and sighed when she realized she awoke to a new morning alone once again. She rolled over on her back and pulled the sheet up around her neck and held back the tears in her eyes as she looked at the ceiling. Just once she wanted to wake up next to him in the morning. All she wanted to do was roll over and lay her head on his sleeping chest when she first awoke.

Once Sydney regained her emotional strength she got out of bed and straightened the covers. She walked through the house feeling the cool air of the morning and wondered if a window was open. When she got in the kitchen she grabbed her pack of cigarettes and lighter and walked out the back door. She pulled a cigarette out of the pack with her lips and lit the end. She inhaled and focused on the amber coals at the end of the stick. She sat down on the wooden chair on the back porch and pulled her feet up in the seat. She placed the cigarette pack and lighter on the arm of the chair and pulled her long shirt over her knees. She watched the morning birds float around the back yard looking for breakfast. She looked at the cigarette and shook her head when she realized this was probably going to be her breakfast for the day.

Sydney held the glowing stick of smoke in her lips as she pulled her hair into a ponytail. When she realized that she did not bring a ponytail holder she let it fall back down behind her. While holding the cigarette between her pointer finger and middle finger she took a long drag with her eyes closed. When her eyes closed, an image of a man came to her mind. The man had piercing green eyes and a firm jaw. She felt her body shiver at the thought of his eyes. There was something about his eyes that was familiar to her. She could feel her heart beat faster and did not understand why. She opened her eyes and took one last drag and dropped the still-burning cigarette into a tin coffee can on the porch.

Before Sydney walked back into the house she blew out the secondhand smoke. She let the screen door slam shut behind her as she walked back into the house to take a shower. She quickly surveyed the room and saw that several of the candles had burnt out during the night. Sydney moved into the bathroom and pulled off her nightshirt and started the hot water in the shower. She placed a towel on a hook by the shower, pulled off her panties and stepped into the shower. The hot water ran over the front of her body and then her back. She closed her eyes and saw the man with the piercing green eyes again. His lips moved and he whispered, "I love you." She smiled and wrapped her arms around her body in a hug.

VIII

Sydney's smile vanished when Kenny walked into her office at the hospital. He walked around to her desk and gave her a peck on her cheek as she typed on the computer.

"Good morning, babe."

Sydney waited two more seconds before pushing away from the computer and turning to look at Kenny to wish him a good morning. "Where did you go this morning?"

Kenny poured himself a cup of coffee and said, "I went to the gym. You know that."

"Yeah I know," she paused and spun a pen on her desk. "Did you ever come to bed last night?"

Kenny half-sat on the corner of the desk as he held the steaming cup of coffee. "Actually no, I slept all night on the recliner." He took a sip of coffee. "It was too comfortable to get up and move."

Sydney looked down at her desk and sighed. Kenny used his free hand to lift her chin. "Babe, what's the matter? You look upset."

She gave him a fake smile and grabbed his hand. "Kenny, why don't you ever want to wake up together in the morning?"

"Oh babe," he said as he leaned forward to give her a gentle kiss on the lips. "You know why I get up early every morning. You know it's important to me."

"I know, but—" Sydney stopped herself.

Kenny rubbed the side of her cheek as he took another sip of coffee. Sydney continued, "I just want it once in a while."

Kenny looked down at her and got serious. He used his hand to turn her face toward his. "Sweetie, do you know how long I lie there and look at you before I leave?"

Sydney blushed, "No," she whispered.

"Sometimes I fear that I may wake you because I stare at you for so long. Every morning before I leave I take a few minutes to admire your beauty before I go."

Sydney stood up from her chair and gave Kenny a hug as he returned the hug with one arm. "I'm sorry, I was just feeling lonely this morning, that's all," apologized Sydney.

Kenny gave her a kiss on the lips and pushed her away. "I need to go, Syd." He walked to the door and turned back to smile at Sydney. "I'll be home late tonight."

Caught off guard, Sydney asked, "What? Why?"

Kenny stopped and turned to look back at her. "You know I have a meeting to attend."

Frustrated, Sydney asked, "What, with that stupid new group you joined? What are they called again? The Seekers or something stupid like that?" She regretted what she was saying but could not control herself. The words poured out of her mouth before she had any time to think of something better to say.

Sydney could see the anger flash across Kenny's face. "Yes, the Seekers and you know I cannot and will not tell you what it is about," he said through tight lips.

They stood staring at each other for a long moment before Kenny broke the silence by asking, "Okay?"

Sydney nodded her head okay and watched him walk out of the office. She wrapped her arms around her chest and mumbled to herself, "I still don't understand."

IX

Jack pulled the throw rug back and lifted the wooden hatch and leaned it against a chair. He dropped two brown sacks down the dark hole and climbed down after them, using the carved stone ladder. The dirt at the base of the ladder crunched under his boots when he reached the bottom. He picked up the two brown sacks and slung them over his shoulder and strolled down the stone tunnel and stopped at the first torch that was burnt out. Jack opened one of the brown sacks and pulled out a container of kerosene. He coated the charred torch with the liquid. With a flick of a wooden match Jack lit the torch and continued down the tunnel. He relit the four torches that lined the stone tunnel to the labyrinth. When he got to the entrance of the labyrinth, he dropped both brown sacks and bowed slightly. He clasped his hands together in a prayer position before his chest and said a silent prayer of thank you to God before entering the sacred space. He relit the nine torches that circled the labyrinth.

As he lit the nine torches, Jack thought back to when he started building the labyrinth under his house. He believed that God had led him to this house for the purpose of building the labyrinth. He had searched for months for a piece of property where he could build a labyrinth. He originally looked out in the country near horse farms.

But the properties were not secluded enough for his purpose. He looked in the mountains. But the terrain was too steep and rocky. Then one day while he was jogging on the bike path that cut through his hometown he took a side road and jogged past a tiny house that was for sale. A voice inside of his head told him to call his realtor immediately. He did. When the realtor showed him the house he was more excited than surprised to find the wooden hatch that led to the bomb shelter. Jack put a bid on the house that afternoon.

It took Jack months to tear out the guts of the bomb shelter. He replaced all of the metal paneling with stone and pulled out all of the electrical wiring and hung the torches. When the space was clear of anything man-made he started on the construction of the labyrinth. He laid the stones in a pattern for a seven-circuit labyrinth. With each stone he placed he gave thanks to God and asked God to bless the purpose of the labyrinth. At each 180-degree turn in the labyrinth he would pause and meditate on the purpose of his endeavor. Eventually he finished his underground labyrinth.

Shortly after buying the house Jack met a female reverend at the library while he was researching the construction of labyrinths. The reverend, Dorothy Taylor, insisted on helping Jack in designing the seven-circuit labyrinth. At first Jack was reluctant for any help. He felt this was a journey that he needed to accomplish on his own. However, Reverend Taylor was persistent. Jack soon learned that the reverend had worked with many cathedrals around the country in constructing labyrinths of similar design. Her most famous labyrinth was an eleven-circuit design within a nondenominational church on the east coast of Canada. Part of the design included a massive, stained-glass window the same size of the labyrinth that hung on the north wall of the church. Therefore, when the sun shone through the stained glass, the labyrinth would be bathed in a rainbow of light during the day. Reverend Taylor preached that the natural spectrum of sunlight embraced the light in each individual's soul.

When Jack relented and shared his idea with the reverend, she was naturally concerned with the location he had chosen. The reverend was concerned that building a labyrinth underground would attract the dark forces of the universe. The thought never occurred to Jack because his intentions stemmed from true love. He felt embarrassed to relay that belief to Reverend Taylor, so instead he explained the tunnels would be lit by torches, and when he meditated in the center, he would be surrounded by candlelight. Eventually Jack shared the poem he had written about his soulmate and how he wanted to use the power of the labyrinth and meditation to reach her again. The reverend smiled and embraced Jack with a hug. She never complained again about the labyrinth being underground.

When the labyrinth was complete the reverend came to visit often and walk its path. She would spend hours praying in the center of the labyrinth while Jack watched. After one session she commented to Jack that it was one of her favorites and she believed one of the most powerful labyrinths she had ever helped design. He asked her why she felt it was powerful. She simply smiled and said, "Because I am able to talk with Jesus when I'm in the center."

X

Sydney stood in the shower and squeezed the bottle of shampoo onto her hand. She brought her hand full of shampoo to her nose and closed her eyes to smell the scent of cucumber and lime. She smiled at the refreshing scent and began to rub the soap over her scalp, working the liquid into her hair. As the lather of the soap built up in her hair she rubbed the lather over her body. She wanted to make sure that the scent was strong on her skin. Sometimes it seemed silly to her, but she wanted to smell good for herself, not for anyone else.

When she finished washing her hair she turned her back to the stream of hot water and tilted her head back. She used her hands to comb out the soap from her hair. She pulled her hair back into a ponytail and squeezed out the rest of the soapsuds and pulled the ponytail over her right shoulder. Before she turned off the water to dry off she brushed her teeth. Kenny thought it was disgusting that she brushed her teeth in the shower and commented that she had to be the only person in the world that he knew of that brushed her teeth in the shower. After that comment Sydney always made it a point to leave her toothbrush and toothpaste in the shower for Kenny to see.

Sydney turned off the water and pulled her fluffy towel off of the hook. She pressed the towel against her face, wiping it dry. Next, she moved the towel down her body to dry her neck, then her breasts and slid the towel down her stomach. She lifted her left foot to the edge of the shower to dry her leg, and then stepped out of the shower into the bathroom once she finished drying her right leg. She dried her back and wrapped the towel around her chest, tucking the corner of the towel in her cleavage. She grabbed a hand towel to wipe off the steam that clung to the mirror.

As Sydney wiped the steam away she saw the reflection of a man with piercing green eyes standing behind her. Her body froze when she saw the reflection. Her mouth partially fell open. Her breathing became short, shallow gasps of air. The man with the piercing green eyes took a step forward, and Sydney could feel his presence directly behind her. As she stared through the mirror at the man, his image faded as the steam clung to the glass again. She quickly wiped the mirror again and he was gone.

Sydney spun on her heels, but she was alone. She grabbed the door handle to the bathroom door and it was still locked. She pulled back the shower curtain and saw nothing. She grabbed the hand towel and wiped down the entire mirror again. Still nothing. She turned and leaned against the sink. She wondered what was wrong with her. What was happening?

***

Jack rose from his kneeling position and took a deep breath through his nose. He savored the scent of cucumber and lime.

XI

Jack's soul hovered in front of the window and did not move as a man walked out of the room. The bedroom was empty with the covers of the bed in disarray. Clothes scattered the floor and several of the drawers in the dresser were half open. One lamp on the bedside table was turned on and several candles were lit on the dresser across the room. The mirror above the dresser reflected the candlelight into the large room.

The bathroom door from the bedroom was closed and a light shone from under the door. Jack assumed his soulmate was in the bathroom getting ready for bed.

The telephone rang and on the third ring he heard the man's voice. "Hello," he paused. "Sure, let me get her." The man yelled from another room of the house, "Sydney, the phone is for you!"

Sydney, thought Jack. His soulmate's name was Sydney.

The bathroom door opened and Sydney crossed the room, wearing a pair of bikini panties and a white tank top. She hopped on the bed and picked up the receiver.

"Hello?" she paused, "Oh, hi Dad, how are you?"

Jack's soul floated outside of the bedroom window and listened.

"I know I didn't call this morning, I was really late for work."

"It's not important why I was late." She paused. "Kenny's fine." She paused again, "Everything is fine between Kenny and me."

Hearing the sound of Sydney's voice filled Jack's soul with a happiness he never imagined. As silly as it seemed, the sound of Sydney's voice was like music to his soul.

Sydney whispered into the telephone receiver, "Dad, I just wish Kenny had more to offer. Look, I don't want to talk about this right now, especially with him home." Sydney took a deep breath. "No, I am not mad at you. I'm frustrated. Not with you. With him."

Jack listened as Sydney paused and listened to whatever her dad was saying on the other end of the phone. She answered, "I don't know. He joined some new group." She paused. "Something called the Seekers for something." She exhaled loudly, "I don't know, Dad. He won't tell me anything about it."

Jack's soul moved to look through the window again at Sydney as she talked on the telephone. He believed he could watch her forever. He had spent so many nights staring at the night sky and the two moons, dreaming of how beautiful she might be. He never imagined the beauty he now saw in front of him.

Jack memorized every detail of Sydney that night. He could almost feel her long hair that draped across her shoulders outlining her face. He wished he could slide his hands along the smooth skin of her legs to feel her slender muscles. His soul fingers twitched at the thought of running his hands over her shoulders and chest that framed the shape of her breasts and stomach in her tank top. To Jack, watching Sydney was pure pleasure.

Jack listened to every word Sydney said while she was on the telephone. He absorbed every pronunciation and every accent in her voice. His eyes became transfixed on her lips as they moved with each word that she spoke. He watched them as they parted and pressed together to form the words and syllables that came from her.

"I know, Dad, and I love you too. Good night," said Sydney as she hung up the phone. Jack watched as she sat on the edge of her bed and looked out the window. For a moment Jack's soul was afraid that Sydney could see him. He held absolutely still and looked into her eyes through the window. He saw that she was sad. Her soul was sad. It was then that Jack sensed that Sydney had settled with the man in the house.

***

Sydney hung up the telephone. She sat on the edge of the bed and saw the twin moons through her window. Her body shivered as if she was being watched, and she leaned closer to the window to peer out of it but saw nothing. She wrapped her arms around her body and looked at the twin moons again and wondered when the next full moons would happen. She shivered again and peered out the window and still saw nothing. She pulled the blinds closed and turned to walk out of the room. She turned off the lamp by the window with the light switch and let the candles continue to burn.

***

Jack's soul pushed back from the window and floated higher into the sky, back to his body.

XII

Sydney closed her eyes and stretched the full length of her body on the bed. She spread her arms and legs like a starfish and partly enjoyed having the whole bed to herself. At the same time she was frustrated because Kenny was gone again. He had left earlier in the evening to attend one of his stupid Seekers of the Whatever meeting. She often wondered why it frustrated her. She was not that happy with him. Maybe it was the fact that she hated to be alone and at least he filled that void. She frowned. It was not nice of her to think in that way. He did have some good traits. Just not traits that fulfilled her.

She straightened her nightshirt and rolled over onto her side to go to sleep. She knew there was no point in staying up for him. He would be home late and would not even try to wake her. She closed her eyes and hoped her dreams would be more fulfilling than her life.

***

Sydney held the sides of her gown as she wiggled her toes in the loose dirt on the ground. The torches did not give off enough light for her to examine her surroundings in detail, so she reached out and felt the stone walls with her fingertips. She pressed the palms of her hands firmly against the rough surface and closed her eyes to feel the earth around her. The wall was cooler than she expected. She moved her face close to the wall and pressed her cheek to the stone, wishing it would speak to her. She wanted the stones to tell her the history and meaning of this place.

The stones remained silent.

Sydney pressed away from the stones and brushed off the specks of dirt that clung to the satin fabric of her nightgown. She then realized that she was wearing a nightgown. She never wore a nightgown. She held the material out from her body and released it to let it fall against her skin. The fabric clung to her body and hugged every curve of her shape. She smiled to herself at how sexy and desirable she felt. Still rubbing the fabric, she walked deeper into the stone tunnel. All of her senses were heightened for any sound, sight, or smell that might catch her attention to give her a clue of where she was. As Sydney walked through the stone tunnel, she did not feel afraid or alone. She felt protected and safe. Everything felt familiar.

The tunnel made a complete ninety-degree turn and opened up to a large, circular room. The room was larger and brighter than the tunnel. Sydney glanced around the room and saw several torches hanging from the walls, burning brightly. On the floor of the circular room she saw a path outlined by stones that twisted and turned. She followed the path with her eyes and in the center of the room a group of white, pillar-shaped candles burned.

Sydney lifted her leg to take a step over a stone to walk to the cluster of candles in the middle, but she stopped in mid-stride. She pulled her foot back and traced the outlined stone path again with her eyes. She whispered, "It's a labyrinth," in amazement.

When Sydney took her next step, it was along the path of the labyrinth. Each step she took was a measured stride. She watched her feet with each step she took. She twisted and turned with each curve of the labyrinth path. With each step she took, the worries of her world floated off of her. With each turn of the path, her soul felt more connected to her heart. When she reached the center of the labyrinth, she knelt among the burning candles. She closed her eyes and felt the room around her swirl. She breathed slowly and felt as if her soul had left her body. Sydney felt as if she were floating on the edge between one reality and the next. She felt that with one thought she could cross over to the next reality. To a world of her choosing. The feeling thrilled her and scared her.

Sydney opened her eyes and before her on the stone floor among the candles she saw the word LOVE carved in the stone. Below that word were more letters that were covered by chips of wax and dirt. She bent forward and brushed the debris away with her hand and revealed her name.

Sydney straightened her back and looked at the two words carved in the stone floor in front of her.

LOVE

SYDNEY

Sydney leaned forward and traced each letter with her fingers. The indentations were real. The letters spelled what she saw. Pressing the palms of both hands on the carved letters, she closed her eyes. This time when she closed her eyes the image of the man with the piercing green eyes flashed in her mind. She gasped, took a quick breath, and opened her eyes. She looked around, thinking she was being watched, and realized that she was physically alone. She leaned forward again and placed her palms on the letters again and closed her eyes. The man with the piercing green eyes reappeared in her mind.

Sydney could clearly see his face, the defined structure of his jaw and cheekbones, and his mesmerizing green eyes. Her hands shook as she pressed her palms harder against the letters on the floor. The man's lips parted and mouthed, "I love you."

Sydney pulled her hands from the carved letters and quickly leaned back on her heels to stand up. She could feel her heart racing and her body flush from the heat coursing through her torso. She stood among the candles and steadied her trembling legs. "How?" she whispered.

***

Jack stood up from his kneeling position at the center of the labyrinth when he felt her presence approach from the stone hallway. He was momentarily confused about how her soul had found him. He was not upset by the turn of events, just confused. He quickly traced his steps out of the labyrinth and moved into the shadows to visibly hide himself from the presence of her soul.

He stood in the shadows of the torches that burned in the circular room of the labyrinth. He watched as Sydney entered the chamber with the labyrinth. He wondered if she would recognize the stone path as a labyrinth. To his delight, she smiled when she traced the path to the center. He watched as Sydney kneeled among the burning candles. He watched as she traced her fingers across the letters that he had so carefully carved into the stone. He wondered if she could feel him in the labyrinth with her. His heart hoped that she would see him. But his heart was also afraid.

Afraid of rejection.

***

Sydney retraced her steps out of the labyrinth. With each step and turn she felt her soul descend back into her body. As she reached the beginning of the labyrinth, she felt her heart and soul pull farther apart. At the entrance of the labyrinth, she felt the gulf between the two realities in her soul. She turned around to look back at the cluster of candles in the center of the labyrinth and thought she saw movement in the shadows by one of the torches. She called out, "Anyone there?"

Nothing answered her.

***

Jack took a step back deeper into the shadows. He suddenly became afraid that Sydney had seen him. When she called out, "Anyone there?" he was unable to answer her. His soul wanted to scream for her. Wanted to scream, "I am here!"

He did not move or answer.

Jack stood silent in the shadows and watched her vanish.

XIII

Sydney jumped when she felt something touch her hand. She opened her eyes and saw her best friend, Nadine, sitting on the edge of her bed. She brought both hands to her eyes and pushed the hair out of her face to catch her breath and asked, “Nadine, what are you doing here?”

“We had breakfast plans, remember?”

“Shit!” Sydney sat up in bed and tried to gather her wits about her. “Can I have a second?”

Nadine smiled and turned to leave the room. When her friend left and closed the door, Sydney lay back in bed and closed her eyes. She revisited her dream and the letters that were carved on the stone floor of the labyrinth. It was a dream she thought. But it felt real. Everything felt real. Even she felt real in the dream. The labyrinth felt real. She felt as if she was actually there in the stone tunnel. She looked at her hands and fingers and they were smudged with dirt. She smiled and glided toward the shower to get ready.

***

When Sydney emerged from the shower she could smell the fresh scent of brewed coffee and hear the sizzle of bacon. She shook her head in disbelief that Nadine was actually making an attempt at breakfast. For a moment she wondered if Kenny was home and he was making breakfast—which made her even more nervous because Sydney knew that Nadine had eyes for Kenny. Sydney didn’t really believe her best friend would betray her in that way. But she didn’t want to tempt fate either. She knew how unhappy Nadine was with Luke.

Sydney quickly got dressed and made her way downstairs. When she walked into the kitchen she was relieved to see that it was just Nadine standing over the sizzling bacon. Sydney asked, "Where's Billy?"

Nadine handed Sydney a cup of coffee, "At his friend's. I figured we needed some girl time alone." She smiled and took a sip of her own coffee.

Sydney glanced down at her coffee and added more cream. She grabbed her cigarettes and made her way out to the back porch. After a few moments Nadine followed Sydney outside with two plates of scrambled eggs and bacon. When Nadine kicked the screen door open Sydney grabbed it and held it open for her friend. She watched Nadine and wondered if Kenny thought she was attractive. Sydney was always jealous of her petite size and knew that most men preferred that over her taller frame and build. Sydney asked, "Do you think Kenny finds you attractive?"

Nadine laughed. "Oh God, are you on that again?"

Sydney looked away and took a puff of her cigarette, more to hide the expression on her face than needing more nicotine. After a moment she shook her head no and asked, "Do you think Luke still finds you attractive?" She looked over at her friend.

Nadine took a slow deliberate bite and chewed it a long time before answering. "At one time, yes." She paused. "But now, I don't know."

Sydney took a sip of her coffee. It was better than it normally was when Nadine brewed it. She looked out toward the forest that bordered her backyard. "I don't think Kenny even thinks I exist anymore."

Nadine nodded her head in agreement, "Luke loves Billy. There is no doubt. He is devoted to him. I am too in my own way. But different than Luke." She paused as if collecting her thoughts. "I think, and Luke would probably agree with me but never say it out loud, we mistook lust for love."

Sydney smiled at her friend. "Don't we all?"

Nadine looked at her with sadness in her eyes, "It's hard, Sydney. Some days I can tolerate him. Other days I can't stand the sight of him and that makes me so sad because he is so wonderful with Billy. He is never mean to me and he tries to be loving toward me. But I am so cold to him that I don't even see his attempts until hours or days later, and then it is too late."

Sydney snuffed out the butt of her cigarette in a can and asked, "Why can't you stand the sight of him?"

Nadine swallowed a bite of eggs. "We have nothing in common. This sounds mean. But when he talks I don't care what he has to say. I love when he leaves to go to the gym or work so I don't have to deal with him and then I dread when he comes home."

"Why don't you leave him?" asked Sydney.

Nadine laughed. "No way. I'm not going through a second divorce."

Sydney remembered Nadine's first marriage. He was a nice guy, but she left him after a few years because he never talked and she was unhappy. She turned and looked at Nadine again in a different light and wondered if maybe she wasn't meant to be with a guy in the first place. Maybe Nadine's soulmate was a female. She smiled at the thought of her best friend being gay. She asked, "Do you believe in soulmates?"

Nadine laughed. "No. All men are the same and want the same thing."

Sydney shrugged and took out another cigarette. "I don't know about that. I don't believe all men are the same."

Nadine kicked at her friend as they sat across from each other. "What are you talking about? Kenny is just like Luke, but different. Kenny is always gone and wants nothing to do with you." She paused. "I wouldn't be surprised if he wasn't getting something on the side, as absent as he is from you physically and emotionally."

Sydney shook her head no. "No, he isn't getting any on the side. He just stretches himself thin and doesn't think time together is important."

Sydney felt her friend's eyes burning into her and refused to turn and look at her. Nadine asked, "Why are you defending him?"

"My mother always said that men needed clubs, projects, and work to keep themselves busy and to feel important," said Sydney.

Nadine laughed. "Well Saint Norma grew up in a time before us and when men were still gentlemen. Things are different."

Sydney smiled at the thought of her mom and continued. "Kenny isn't that bad. He provides for me. We do get along. Sex isn't bad when it happens." She paused and looked off to the forest again.

Nadine continued Sydney's thought. "But something is missing."

Sydney nodded her head in acknowledgment.

Nadine looked out toward the forest and stated, "Maybe that's life. Something will always be missing."

Before thinking, Sydney whispered, "That's sad."

The two friends sat in silence for a while, drinking their coffee and letting breakfast go cold. They chitchatted for a bit about various topics, but nothing as complicated as relationships. Sydney felt as if a sadness of some kind had descended over them and was refusing to leave. She didn't understand how Nadine felt about Luke and knew that Nadine didn't understand her about Kenny. But they were friends, and she knew that was more important than anything else. She reached over and squeezed Nadine's hand. Nadine looked at her and smiled at her with sad eyes.

"Try to find the goodness in Luke. He's not a bad guy and isn't bad to look at either," she said with a smile.

Nadine pulled her hand back in shocked surprise and tried not to laugh. "I knew it! You do have the hots for Luke!"

Sydney barked a short laugh and blushed. "No."

Nadine squinted her eyes at Sydney. "But there is someone," she pressed.

Sydney looked away from her friend and thought about her dreams and all the experiences she had had lately. Even if she wanted to tell Nadine about them, she didn't know how. Even to herself all of her experiences sounded crazy. Without looking at her friend, Sydney said, "There is no one else." She turned to look at Nadine. "I think I spend so much time dreaming of my soulmate that at times I think he is real and comes to me in my dreams." She blushed. "Which is as silly as a little girl wanting to be rescued by a knight in shining armor."

Nadine smiled at her friend. "You have been dreaming of your soulmate since we were kids." She stood and leaned over to kiss Sydney on the top of the head and whispered, "That's what's missing; Kenny isn't your soulmate. And that is what you have always compared him to: your imaginary soulmate."

The screen door to the house slammed shut behind Nadine as she walked back into the kitchen. Sydney stared out at the forest and exhaled deeply. She knew Nadine was right.

XIV

The pavement passed under Jack's feet as they pounded the ground with each step he took. Pushing himself, he wanted to feel the burn in his lungs and in his leg muscles as he pushed his body to its limits. He wanted to make himself better. He wanted to sweat out the impurities in his soul. He wanted to outrun his fears. The lights in the homes he passed beckoned for him to ask, "What are they doing up so late?" The lights called to him to peer into their lives and watch the show they had to display.

He could see the self-imposed finish line just ahead of him. He lengthened his stride to move faster to push his body past its limits. He crossed the imaginary finish line and could hear the crowd cheering. He slowed to a walk and calmed his breathing as he walked up the path to his house.

Inside the house Jack grabbed a towel and wiped the sweat off of his face and neck. He pulled open the wooden hatch and descended into the tunnel. He quickly walked down the tunnel to the entrance of the labyrinth. He knelt in a prayer position at the entrance and bowed his head. Jack said a long, silent prayer to God to give him the strength to follow his heart, the courage to stand strong in his beliefs, and for forgiveness for the transgressions he had committed in his lifetime. When he was finished he stood and walked the path of the labyrinth to the center.

XV

Sydney sat on the back steps of her porch in the twin moonlight with a white silk wrap curled around her body. The night air was cool and still, which caused a layer of fog to settle in the backyard. She brought her cigarette to her lips and took a puff and held the smoke in her lungs. She let the smoke out and watched a squirrel dart across the yard and disappear into the fog. She pulled her knees close to her body and wrapped both arms around her knees to rest her chin. The only time she lifted her head was to take a puff of her cigarette. She did not feel cold from the weather, but she found herself rubbing her bare legs with her hands to give her hands something to do. With her head resting on her knees, she stared out into the backyard and let her eyes mist over in thought.

Sydney thought about her life. She thought about her job at the hospital. She enjoyed helping her patients. Her uncle always believed that her hands were capable of healing anyone. She wanted to believe so bad that she had healing hands. She wanted to believe that she had something special to offer the world. At times when she did help someone in need, she felt special, but the times of that happening were few and far between. She did not even know how she had ended up as a nurse to begin with. It was not her dream as a child to work in a hospital full of germs and sick people. She wanted to be an ice princess. She wanted to twirl on the ice and feel her body fly through the air as she leapt from the ice. It took her years to come to the realization that some dreams never come true.

Sydney thought about how she lived in a suburb on the edge of a city and lived a dull life like everyone else. Tears stung her eyes and she closed them tight. She did not know why she was so upset. In reality she had nothing to be upset about. She knew she had a good life. She was raised by great parents. Married to a man that loved her and had a good job. But she felt so empty.

Alone.

Sydney always felt that she was looking for something. Looking for the purpose of her life. Or looking for the one person that understood her without her having to say a word.

Sydney sniffed as a few tears rolled down her cheeks and hit the treated wood of the porch. She did not make a move to wipe the tears from her face or stop crying. She closed her eyes and let the tears fall from her face.

***

Jack knelt on the stone floor and could feel Sydney's sadness emitting from her soul. He floated over the distance to try to understand her sadness. When he reached her soul, she was in a dark box with one small hole of light penetrating the box. He looked in through the hole and saw her sitting with her knees drawn to her chest, her arms wrapped around her lower legs, and her head resting on her knees. Jack could hear the soft whimpers of her cries. He laid his body across the top of the box and his head on the metal lid pressing his ear to the cold metal. He closed his eyes and prayed to God for understanding of Sydney's pain.

***

Jack opened his eyes when he finished his prayer and found he stood on a pile of leaves lying in the grass. His vision was blurred from the layer of fog that shrouded him. In the distance he could hear Sydney crying. He moved toward the sound of her wet sniffles until he walked out of the fog and stood only feet from her sitting on the back porch. He looked up in the cloudy sky and watched the clouds pass over the two moons. He looked back at Sydney and saw that she was shivering, but he did not think she noticed. Jack stepped closer to Sydney and squatted in front of her. He wondered if she knew that he was there, if she could feel him. He watched as her tears rolled down her soft cheeks and struck the ground beneath her.

Sydney raised her head and looked at Jack.

***

Sydney lifted her head from her knees and looked out into the backyard. Several tears ran down her cheeks when she moved her head. The fog in her backyard had gotten thicker and more clouds had rolled past the twin moons. She rested her head back on her knees and closed her eyes again. Several more tears ran down her cheeks and fell from the ridge of her jawbone.

***

Jack watched as the tears rolled down Sydney's cheek and dangled from the ridge of her jawbone. He reached out with his hand and watched as the tears dropped onto his fingertips. The tears bubbled on his fingertip and a couple dripped off his nail. Jack brought his fingertip to his lips and tasted Sydney's tears with the tip of his tongue. Her tears molded to the shape of his tongue as they were absorbed into his mouth. He closed his lips around his finger and smiled at the salty taste of her tears. He closed his eyes with his fingertip in his mouth and stood from his squatted position.

The fog moved in closer to Jack and wrapped its white blanket around his body. He could feel the strength of the fog tug at his soul to bring him back. He willingly let the fog pull his soul to his body in the labyrinth as he cherished Sydney's tears on his tongue.

***

Sydney raised her head after a few minutes and saw that the fog had lifted and the twin moons were high in the sky. She could not explain how or why, but she felt better. She no longer felt so alone. She looked up at the twin moons and smiled. She rose from the steps of the back porch and wiped the remainder of the tears from her eyes before walking back into the house.

XVI

Jack walked out the front door and sat on the porch. He looked up at the two moons in the sky and said out loud, "I must be with her."

XVII

Sydney sat across the table from Kenny and watched his lips move but heard nothing he said. He had been rambling all through dinner about his business trip. A part of her wondered if he really had gone on a business trip for work or if he did something else when he was away. Something just did not make sense to her. He had never gone on a business trip before. She shrugged the thought off because it really did not matter to her. She wondered if he missed her. He never showed it.

Kenny paused his speech when they both heard the roar of thunder outside of their house.

Kenny looked at Sydney. "We're supposed to have a major storm tonight."

"Oh."

"Do we have candles in case we lose power?" asked Kenny.

Sydney gave him a stupid look and chuckled. "What do you think?"

"What? I'm just asking," replied Kenny. "Geez."

Sydney took her third bite of food that had been pushed around her plate for the past half-hour. She looked down at her plate to hide the frown on her face. Kenny really did not know her, she realized once again. She looked up at him with a disappointed look on her face and then the doorbell rang. They both looked at each other, wondering who was coming to visit. Kenny made no movement to get the door. Irritated, Sydney pushed back her chair and left the kitchen.

Sydney's father always taught her to look out the window before she opened the door at night. This time she did not. She opened the door and the man with the piercing green eyes stood on her front porch. She stared at him for the longest time, wondering if she was dreaming or if this was real. She was frozen in place, unable to speak or move. Her knees became weak and she was unsure if she could remain standing. Her heart beat faster and she felt as if she would lose control of her breath. She grasped the doorknob even tighter with her sweaty palm. She wanted to look away, but her eyes were locked on his.

A smile stretched across his perfect lips and she felt her soul leap out to his. She was drawn to him. She could feel the tug of his soul against hers. It took all of her physical power and control to stand her ground and not get lost in his arms. She watched as the man with the piercing green eyes reached his hands out to her.

To go to him.

To join him as one.

Sydney's soul took control of her body and stepped through the doorway and pulled the door closed behind her. The latch of the lock never clicked and her hand lingered on the metal doorknob.

They stood only inches from each other, each staring into the other's eyes. Their breathing became rhythmic. Their hearts skipped a beat. Their souls vibrated with excitement.

The smile on her lips faded as she whispered, "I can't."

Her head turned, breaking eye contact. She pushed the door open with her butt and walked back into the house. She closed the door and the latch clicked. She rested her head against the thick wood of the door and tears streamed down her cheeks.

***

Thunder cracked and lightning danced across the sky. Rain started to fall as a drizzle at first and turned into a downpour as the seconds passed. Jack took several steps back in shocked horror at what had just happened. His soul crushed. He stood in the rain and watched the window in the front door. He could see the top of her head and waited to see her eyes once again.

***

Sydney took a deep breath and prayed that the man with the piercing green eyes was gone. She looked through the small window in the door and saw him standing in the rain. She reached up and clawed the window with her fingernails, wanting to run to him, but was frozen with her tears dripping from her chin onto the hardwood floor. Sydney was unable to look away from the man with the piercing green eyes as he stood in the rain staring back at her with sadness filling his eyes. Her sobs of sorrow escaped her lips uncontrollably.

***

Jack watched as Sydney clawed at the small window. The rain continued to come down in sheets from the sky and drenched him. He stood unfazed by the cold water. He was unable to speak or move. The only response from his body was the uncontrollable tears that fell from his eyes and mixed with the rain puddles on the ground. He stood there wanting her to want him. He hoped and prayed she would open the door and bring him in from the rain. With a flash of lightning, Jack understood. The time was not right for her to let go and be with him. Her heart was too loving and caring to turn her back on any creature that needed her. The time was not right for their love to grow together in a reality that they both wanted so badly.

Jack realized what he wanted was unfair to Sydney, that his wish for their love to become real without her consent was a violation to her being and to their love. He closed his eyes and let the tears run down his face as he felt the rain strike his head and shoulders. He turned on his heels and walked away from his one true love.

Book IV

Cora rolled in bed and opened her eyes to a purple sky and golden wheat stalks. She closed her eyes and felt a gentle hand rub her bare back. She turned her head to the side and opened her eyes a second time and saw Lance sitting on the edge of her bed rubbing her back.

"Hi," whispered Lance as he brushed her auburn hair out of her face.

Cora blinked her eyes but said nothing. She rolled on her back and pulled her covers closer to her chin.

"We need to talk," said Lance.

"Why am I here?" asked Cora. "I thought it was over."

"Please, they are waiting for you," said Lance as he raised his hand to the distant hilltops.

Cora looked up at the two moons that hung in the purple sky. She rose from her bed, wrapped the sheet around her nude body, and walked through the wheat field. She turned her head back to see if Lance was following her. He was gone. With a tinge of disappointment, she continued to glide toward the distant hilltops. She felt the soft wind blow through her hair and the grains of the wheat stalks brush against her bare arms. She glided up a hillside and found two men in dark purple cloaks waiting for her. One was Lance. The older man Cora guessed was Gavin.

"Cora, we're sorry to bring you back," said Gavin.

"I thought it was over," said Cora.

"So did we," responded Lance. "But we found a place that remained hidden even from us.

Gavin motioned for Cora to step higher on the ridge and peer over the side. As she did, she gasped at the horror she saw in the valley below them.

Human bodies were scattered throughout the valley in torturous positions. In the middle of the valley, a man hung from a cross with only a loincloth to cover him. A child hung between four great trees with each limb strung to the trees. A woman was bound and gagged with her body stretched over a boulder. Cora closed her eyes to the pain and sorrow she felt coming from the valley. She turned away in disgust to Lance and Gavin.

She whispered, "Who are they?"

"Victims. Human souls captured by the Myst," said Gavin.

"How? I thought they were all dead," said Cora.

"The last of the Myst," said Lance.

Cora then realized what Lance meant. "You mean the one that fled? The one that killed Lance?"

"Yes," answered Gavin. "But Lance was not killed. Just separated from his physical body," he said as he looked to Lance.

Cora mustered the courage in her soul and looked out to the valley again. The pain and misery from each soul in the valley pleaded for help. Cora took a step forward to race down the hillside to free them from their bondage. Lance placed his hand on her upper arm and gave her pause. She looked back into his eyes and saw that he understood what she felt, understood her need to free the souls so they could begin again.

Gavin spoke behind Lance, "We have already tried."

Cora wheeled on Gavin and stepped up to him. "How can one Myst have so much control in our world?" she asked with an angry tone. She knew she was not mad at Gavin or Lance, but she could not control the rage that she felt inside of her.

Lance gently squeezed Cora's arm to get her attention. "We share this world with all who can journey here." Lance paused until Cora looked at him. "Unfortunately, we do not understand all of the powers of this world with the purple sky."

Gavin continued, "We suspect this is the valley where the Myst hide the souls of the bodies they inhabit."

Lance turned Cora to face him. "We need your help."

Without hesitation Cora answered, "Of course."

Lance smiled. "I need you to recover my body, take it somewhere safe."

Confused, Cora asked, "Why? I can handle it."

Lance's smiled faded. "I'm afraid you can't. This last Myst is too powerful for just one of us. We have to do this together."

Cora looked out over the valley again and nodded her head in agreement.

"I will need my body to fight this last Myst and his soul-lineage in the physical world as well as this world," explained Lance.

Gavin spoke up. "My body has been unoccupied for far too long to be of any use. I will stay here in this world, while Lance returns to yours."

"We also fear that this Myst has found a way to detach its soul-lineage after it has implanted a host," said Lance.

The realization struck Cora immediately. "So killing this Myst may not end it for good?"

Gavin sadly nodded his head in acknowledgment. "This last Myst is one of the original nine that came to our world. For reasons unknown, each of the original nine were capable of being linked to each of their lineage. Which in turn meant they were linked to each human host like a spider's web." Gavin looked out over the valley of torture and continued. "We learned that if one of the original nine were killed, then all of the lineage connected to that original Myst would die."

Gavin closed his eyes. "Sadly, the human hosts linked through that soul-lineage also died." Gavin opened his tear-filled eyes. "At least their souls were free to begin again with God's grace."

Lance continued, "If this last Myst has found a way to unlink itself from each of its lineage, then we would have to kill each individual Myst."

"Which is near impossible," said Cora.

"Exactly," said Gavin. "We would have failed."

Lance cleared his throat. "But God gave us the power to liberate our world." He looked at Cora. "Do you remember where my physical body is buried?"

"Of course."

***

Cora awoke with a start and sat up in bed. With her eyes open in her dark room she watched as the tortured souls floated past her vision. She could see the pain and anguish on each of their faces. Their bodies were twisted, contorted, and were bound in ways that were unthinkable to her. She could hear their pleas for freedom in her mind.

Cora turned and looked out the window at the two moons. She remembered the night the second moon became visible to all of humanity. She thought the fight was over. She believed she was free. But her mind never let her forget the battles she had fought or the innocent souls she had freed by causing their deaths by her hand. She tried to forget. Tried to push the memories away in her heart to where she could no longer feel them. But her actions as one of God's Liberators were too tightly bound to her soul to be able to forget or hide who she was inside of her soul.

Cora climbed out of bed and got dressed in the dark. She walked out of her house and into the rain. She locked the door closed. She bounced her house and car keys in the palm of her hand and had a sense that she would never be returning. She turned and faced the woods that lined her house and threw the keys as hard and far as she could. She pulled the hood of her jacket over her head and walked out into the dark night.

***

"Dammit! I'm so sick of this fucking rain!" yelled Kenny as he slapped the windowpane.

Sydney looked up from her book and choked back the tears that she felt rising to her eyes. Kenny turned around and paced across the room and spit into the dirty fireplace that he refused to clean.

He turned to Sydney. "You know this fucking rain didn't start until that night when that guy came over."

Looking up from her book, she said, "What guy?"

"Beats the shit out of me. You wouldn't tell me," said Kenny as he walked back to the window.

Sydney looked back at the pages of her book but could not see the words through the tears in her eyes. She knew whom Kenny was talking about. What day the rain started. Sometimes at night when she slept alone, she felt the man with the piercing green eyes sitting next to her, playing with her hair. When she dreamed, she often saw him in the distance watching her. A few times he approached and would touch her in the most loving of ways.

"Dammit, it feels like it has been raining forever," snapped Kenny as he left the room.

A tear escaped Sydney's eyes and splattered on the book page sitting in her lap. She closed her eyes and tilted her head back in hopes that the rest of the tears would recede back into her eyes.

***

Kenny pulled the shades closed in the bedroom and turned on the radio loud enough to drown out the raindrops that continuously fell on the roof. He lay in bed staring at the ceiling, cursing under his breath at how miserable his life had become. He wished his time would come. He wished the purpose of the Seekers of the Liberators would make itself known so he could fulfill his purpose in this miserable life.

He closed his eyes and slept.

***

The silver creature strode through the golden wheat stalks to stand before Kenny. The creature reached out with its long, three-fingered arm and grabbed Kenny's throat. It lifted Kenny off the ground to look into his eyes without having to bend at the waist.

Kenny did not struggle. The time had come. Everything he had been taught with the Seekers was coming true. He had finally been chosen to serve.

The silver creature pushed a single thought into Kenny's mind.

Kenny whispered the thought. "Myst."

The silver creature pulled Kenny closer to its face to allow Kenny to look into its golden eyes. Then the creature let go of Kenny and he fell into blackness.

***

Billy pushed his window open and pulled the hood of his jacket over his head. He climbed out on the roof of his parents' house and scooted his way over to the pine tree and climbed down to the ground. It was natural for him to wear a rain suit every day and night just as it was natural for a teenage boy to sneak out of his parents' house in the middle of the night. For as long as he could remember, it had rained. His father often commented that the rain had lasted longer than the flood recorded in the Bible.

From what Billy remembered of Bible class, God had destroyed the world with that flood. God had also promised not to destroy the world by water a second time. Sometimes Billy wondered if God had forgotten his promise to the world.

School had been cancelled for longer than Billy could remember because of flooding. Every week the news channels threatened that school would start soon. But every day they remained closed. Most of Billy's friends hated going out in the rain. They hated getting wet. Billy hated staying inside and not enjoying the beauty of nature, even if everything was wet.

His mother hated him going out in the rain. She always said, "You'll get sick playing in the rain."

"Mom, armies march in the rain and they never get sick," Billy would argue.

"You're not an army," his mother would say in a smartass tone.

His mother would put up a fuss but she never stopped him from playing outside. She was a mom. It was her job to worry.

The rain fell as hard as always and Billy did not avoid the puddles in the street. He made sure to walk through every puddle no matter how deep the water. He came to a short stone wall and hopped over the stones and landed in a mud puddle on the other side. He stood in the mud and looked up at the night sky and saw the two moons playing hide-and-go-seek with the rain clouds.

The moonlight illuminated enough of the graveyard for him to not trip over the smaller tombstones. He always came to the graveyard alone. He felt solace there and besides, his friends were too afraid. He had heard rumors from the older kids that a satanic cult used the graveyard as their meeting place. The same older kids also teased that several local kids his age had disappeared or been sacrificed whenever they got too close to the outer stone wall.

Billy believed the rumors he heard because he had found artifacts and bones in different locations throughout the graveyard that would support such stories of a satanic cult. But it did not scare him enough to stop him from returning whenever he could. Billy enjoyed reading the history of the dead on their tombstones. He enjoyed the small glimpse into someone's life that had been lived so long ago. Sometimes when he was lucky, he thought he had seen spirits and ghosts of those that had crossed over walking through the cemetery.

That evening he felt extremely lucky when he watched two large gargoyles climb down from the roof of a tomb that sat in the middle of the cemetery. He supposed that he should have been shocked to see the gargoyles. However, occurrences like moving stone statues, imaginary friends, and monsters under the bed had been a part of his life since he was three years old, according to his dad. It took Billy a few moments to realize they were gargoyles and not humans. He had heard stories from his parents and neighbors of stone statues coming to life, but he had never experienced it himself. When the gargoyles started to move, Billy crouched behind a large tombstone and watched as the two creatures walked through the cemetery. One of the gargoyles had a wing tip that was chipped off, and he anxiously looked around. The second gargoyle paid no attention to its surroundings and plodded forward in the rain and mud.

Billy stayed low to the ground and behind the tombstones as he followed the two gargoyles. They traveled toward the older section of the cemetery, the section where the forest had begun to grow around the tombstones: the area where the satanic cult was last seen, according to the rumors. The two stone creatures entered the tree line and perched themselves on two crosses as if to get a better view of the tombstones. Billy quietly worked his way closer to the gargoyles and heard a voice.

"Grumly and Bozz, I've missed you," said a female voice.

The gargoyle with the chipped wing tip jumped off of its perch and moved closer to the voice. Billy rose on his knees and peered over the tombstone he hid behind. He watched as the gargoyle lowered its head and let the person with the female voice rub the top of its head. The person stood in a hole with the shovel resting against the side of the hole.

"Bozz, would you care to help me?" asked the person, who Billy assumed was a woman.

The gargoyle with the chipped wing jumped into the hole and the woman grabbed the shovel. Grumly, the gargoyle still perched on the cross, continued to survey the cemetery.

Billy watched as the woman and the gargoyle pitched mud and dirt out of the hole, never stopping to take a break. He crawled on his hands and knees to get closer. His rain suit and face were covered with mud. He looked up at the sky and could tell the sun would be rising soon. No one worked at the cemetery anymore, but Billy wondered what this woman would do when morning arrived.

Billy had worked himself between several tombstones and lay in a good position to be able to confirm that the person was a woman. The hood of her rain poncho was pulled up over her head, but he could see wisps of wet auburn hair trying to escape from the hood. He rose on his elbows to see if Grumly was still perched on the cross. But the gargoyle was gone. Before Billy could move again, Grumly dropped out of the sky and landed with a splatter of mud in front of Billy. Both of its clawed feet pressed into the mud, and its outstretched wings momentarily deflected the rain off of Billy.

Grumly reached down and grasped Billy around the back of the neck and raised him off the ground to toss him toward the open grave. Billy struck the ground hard and slid in the mud toward the woman and the other gargoyle. The woman threw a shovel full of mud on top of Billy before she realized what she did. Bozz jumped out of the grave and stood between Billy and the woman. Grumly leapt back on his cross and turned his back to the grave.

Billy shook his head and wiped the mud off of his face. He pushed up to his knees and looked up at the eyes of the gargoyle. Its breath was foul and the rain dripped off of its leathery skin.

"Who are you?" asked the woman.

"No one," said Billy.

The woman smiled. "Back off, Bozz."

Bozz growled and reluctantly backed away from the boy and stood to the side of the woman. Billy could feel the other gargoyle, Grumly, staring down upon him through the corner of his eye.

The woman leaned against the edge of the grave, "Does 'no one' have a name?"

Billy sat up straight on his knees. "Billy. Billy Rueben."

The woman laughed. "You have to be kidding."

"No, I'm serious," said Billy. "Why do you laugh?"

Cora smiled. "My mom loved eating Reubens. I always thought they were gross."

Billy's eyebrows creased together in slight confusion and he wondered if she was making fun of him or not. He asked, "What's your name?"

"Cora," she said as she pulled herself out of the grave. She stood and looked down at the casket in the hole. "Grumly, Bozz, can you get the body please?"

Billy stood up and tried to wipe the mud off of his rain suit. The two gargoyles moved into the open grave. Cora walked over to him and pulled off her gloves.

"I am so sick of this rain," commented Cora as if they had been friends for years.

Billy just stared at her.

"I need someplace to put this body," said Cora.

"You're asking me?" asked Billy.

"Yes."

"Why?" asked Billy.

Cora placed her hand on his shoulder. "I need your help."

"Why me?" asked Billy.

Cora exhaled. "Because Billy, if you are out skulking around abandoned graveyards in the middle of a stormy night, I am going to assume you are a mischievous little boy or bored out of your mind." She paused. "And whichever is the case, my gut instincts tell me you can help."

Billy looked past Cora and watched as Grumly and Bozz finished wrapping the body from the casket in a plastic tarp and lifted it off the ground. The rain trapped in the tarp escaped out of the folds and poured onto the ground.

Still watching the gargoyles, Billy said, "Um, well there is one place I know of that is not far from here."

***

Kenny woke from his dream in a cold sweat. The bed sheets were wet from his sweat and tangled around his body. He was momentarily unaware what time of day it was. He shuffled out to the kitchen and found Sydney sleeping on the couch. He purposely made excessive noise in the kitchen to wake her up. He hated that she never slept in the bed anymore.

Sydney walked into the kitchen and pulled her zipper hoodie closed when she saw Kenny. Kenny was making the coffee and she asked, "Are you making the cinnamon coffee?"

"No," said Kenny.

Sydney frowned and pulled two coffee mugs out of the cabinet. She stood next to Kenny and rubbed his back with her hand as she scooped sugar into her mug. Kenny walked over to the back door and slapped the windowpane of the door.

"It's still fucking raining out there," he said.

Sydney sighed and leaned against the counter. Kenny turned around and leaned against the back door. He looked at Sydney with tinted golden eyes.

Sydney stepped forward and placed one hand on his cheek and her other hand brushed the hair off of his forehead and felt for a temperature.

"Do you feel okay, honey?" asked Sydney.

"I feel fine. Why?"

Sydney used her fingers to pull both of his lower eyelids down to see more of his eyes. The whites of his eyes were golden, but his irises were still blue. Kenny pulled his head away.

"What are you doing?" he asked.

"Sorry, you crabass, you look sick," said Sydney.

"I am fine," replied Kenny as he stormed out of the kitchen.

***

Kenny walked past the hallway mirror, and unbeknownst to him the reflection of a silver Myst passed in the mirror, and not his own.

***

Billy scraped the mud on the ground with his rubber boot until he found a piece of knotted rope. He bent over, grasped the rope, and pulled. He struggled. Slowly a wooden hatch lifted a couple inches off of the ground. The gargoyle Grumly reached its fingers between the wood and mud and lifted it further with ease. Billy and Grumly dropped the hatch on the mud-soaked ground with a splat. Rain and mud poured down into the black hole.

Cora took a step closer and looked down into the hole. She looked at Billy. "What is it?"

Billy shrugged his shoulders. "Not sure. A friend of my dad's said there used to be a house here."

Cora looked around and did notice the remains of a brick foundation and a crumbling fireplace. "Maybe a basement?" she said, more to herself than anyone else.

"They called it a bomb shelter," corrected Billy.

"A bomb shelter," repeated Cora as she looked in the black hole again. "Have you ever been down there?"

"No," said Billy.

Cora looked at Billy. "What? I could never get the wooden hatch open by myself and my dumb friends are too afraid," defended Billy.

Bozz shifted and moved toward the opening. Cora reached out a hand to stop him, "Hold on, big fella." Bozz snorted in impatience.

Billy pulled out a flashlight and turned it on to illuminate the hole. Against one edge was what looked like a stone ladder carved into the side of the hole. Cora stepped to the ladder and climbed down into the hole as Billy angled the flashlight beam toward the bottom for her. She reached the bottom and stood in the fresh mud that had fallen into the hole when they opened it. She stepped deeper into what looked like a tunnel to get away from the falling rain. She pushed back her hood and shook her mane of hair. Billy descended the ladder, followed by Bozz and Grumly with the body.

"Wow you have a lot of hair," commented Billy.

Cora smiled and turned back to look at him. "You couldn't wait until I told you it was safe?"

Bozz shook his head no. Billy laughed. "Sorry the rain was getting to us."

Cora smiled and squatted to the ground to feel it. It was stone. She rubbed the dirt from the stone between her fingers as she stood. When she stood she saw a torch on the stone wall. She moved and pulled it off the wall and smelled it.

"What are you doing? asked Billy.

"It's a torch," answered Cora. "It smells like kerosene. But who knows how long it has been sitting down here."

Billy pulled off his pack from his shoulders and dug out a lighter and handed it to Cora. She looked at him. "Do you always carry lighters?"

"I'm a boy," smiled Billy. "Of course I do."

Cora flicked the lighter and a small flame ignited. She held it to the old torch and listened as the small flame snapped and cracked, trying to ignite the torch. She leaned forward and gently blew on the red embers on the torch. With a sudden intensity the torch blossomed to life. Cora pulled her face away and moved in a circle to survey their surroundings.

The torch crackled and popped in Cora's hand. "Wait here this time." Billy and the two gargoyles stood just inside of the tunnel away from the falling rain. He watched as Cora walked deeper into the tunnel. He watched as she reached up and held the torch above her head. A second flame ignited against the wall. Cora walked back toward them.

"There seem to be more torches along the wall," said Cora. "Grumly, close the hatch please."

Grumly walked back into the falling rain and jumped up through the hole to the surface. A moment later he was in the tunnel again with the hatch closed. The darkness closed in on the group. Billy took a step closer to Cora. She smiled down at him.

"Grumly, you are in the rear." She looked at Billy. "You behind me."

Billy nodded in agreement.

With Cora in the lead, the group moved through the tunnel. When Cora saw a torch on the wall, she would light it with the flame of the torch she held. Not all of the torches would light. But enough lit for the group to see where they were going. The stone tunnel turned abruptly ninety degrees and opened up into a large space. Cora paused and used her free hand to hold Billy back.

She leaned her head toward his. "Wait here." She looked toward Grumly and jerked her head for him to follow her.

Cora reached out her right hand and felt for the stone wall. Using the wall as a guide, she moved around the open space with Grumly next to her on the left. Every so often Cora would light another torch. Eventually Cora and Grumly worked their way around the entire open space to meet Billy and Bozz again at the entrance of the stone tunnel.

"Nine," said Billy.

Cora looked at Billy. "Nine what?"

"Torches," he said, looking back into the open space. "You lit nine torches that hung on the walls."

The group looked out toward the open space and watched as the room became brighter with the torchlight. As the room got brighter, they could make out a stone path in the center of the room. Cora stepped closer to the stone path and held her torch high above her.

"A labyrinth," she whispered.

Billy stepped up next to her. "What's a labyrinth?"

Cora looked down at Billy. "Um, sort of like a maze, but not really."

Billy cocked his head to the side. "What does that mean?"

Cora looked out toward the stone path and followed it with her eyes, "A maze is designed to have dead ends or tricks to confuse the person walking the path." She paused and tried to make out what was in the center of the labyrinth. "But a labyrinth is one continuous path to the center."

Billy looked out at the stone path. "What's the fun in that?"

Cora smiled and looked back at him, "A labyrinth is not meant to be fun," she looked back out toward the center. "It's meant to be a tool."

"A tool for what?" asked Billy.

"A tool for enlightenment," she whispered.

Billy took a step forward onto the path. "I don't get it." But Cora stopped him by placing her hand on his shoulder. "With each twist and turn of the path, a person's soul transcends higher toward what they believe is their higher power. Once in the middle. . ." she trailed off.

Billy looked at her. "Once in the middle, what?" he asked impatiently.

"Once in the middle the person makes contact with their higher power or their higher intentions," she said, looking back at him.

Billy smiled. "Oh, so it's like a metaphysical thing?"

Cora smiled and shoved him. "No it's more than that."

They both stopped laughing and looked out toward the center of the labyrinth. Both gargoyles stood behind them waiting. Grumly stood guard and Bozz continued to hold the body wrapped in the tarp.

Billy broke the silence first. "What is your higher power," whispered Billy.

"God."

Billy looked at Cora and back to the labyrinth. "Mine too."

Cora turned and looked at him and smiled. She could tell by his answer and body language that he was not one hundred percent sure in that answer. She could not blame him. When she was that age, she did not even know who God was. Now she depended on him for everything. She squatted down and rubbed her hands in the dirt and felt the dry grit against her skin. She whispered, "Why here?"

Billy answered, "Because you said you needed a place to keep the body." He paused. "It was the only place I could think of."

Cora smiled and said, "I was actually asking God why he brought me here. Or why he picked me for this journey."

Billy looked confused. "Picked you for what?"

She wanted to tell him. She wanted to tell him about Lance and Gavin. She wanted to tell him about the Myst and God's Liberators. Instead she smiled at him. He was young. She could tell his soul was experienced. But his physical mind would not understand. She placed her arm around his shoulders and pulled him into a sideways hug.

She pressed her lips to the top of his head and mumbled, "For everything."

Cora dropped her arm and turned to face Bozz and Grumly. Looking at Grumly she said, "Stay here and guard the entrance. I don't think they will find us, but just in case."

Billy interrupted, "Who?"

Cora looked at him and said, "The Myst," and then looked back to Bozz.

"Who are the Myst?" asked Billy.

Cora ignored Billy's question. She reached out and touched one of the gargoyle's shoulders and said, "Bozz, I need you to carry the body to the center." Bozz growled in acknowledgment.

Billy stepped up to Cora, "Who is the Myst?"

Cora looked at him and decided she did not have the time to explain. "I know it is a lot," she paused, "but please trust me." She turned and started to walk the path of the labyrinth.

Bozz followed her, carrying the body. Billy shrugged and followed Bozz.

The three of them walked the labyrinth path in silence. When they reached the center, Cora kicked away old burned candles that were in the center and motioned for Bozz to lay the body down. Cora watched as Billy leaned over and brushed dirt away from the stone floor, where he was going to sit. When the dust cleared she saw the word Love and the name Sydney carved into the stone. She stopped Billy from sitting on top of the words and motioned for him to sit next to the words. To her, it felt more respectful to not cover the words. Cora instructed Bozz to begin unwrapping the body from its plastic covering.

Billy asked, "Who is he?"

"Lance Juddit."

Billy's eyes grew large. "Wait a second," he said.

Cora looked at him. "What?"

"Does he have anything to do with the space program?" asked Billy.

Cora sighed. "Yes."

"Really?"

"Yes. In a roundabout way he is the reason the second moon became visible," answered Cora.

Billy's eyes grew even wider as he connected more pieces to the puzzle, "And the Myst are the aliens that the crew of Juddit III found on the second moon?"

"Yes," Cora stated simply.

Billy's lips spread across his entire face. "You mean I am in the middle of saving the world from an alien invasion?" he asked excitedly.

Cora and Bozz exchanged looks and she answered him, "Sure, if that's what you want to believe."

"Holy shit," he mumbled to himself with the world's largest smile on his face.

Cora sat next to Lance's body in the torch light. She brushed the hair from his face and traced a scar that ran across his cheek and forehead. To her surprise, his skin felt warm. She moved her hand down and touched any skin that was exposed. His neck and hands also felt warm. Cora moved back to touch his face again and realized how handsome he was. She felt something stir inside of her. She had not known him in the physical world, but if she had she would have been attracted to him.

Billy intruded on her thoughts. "Now what?"

"We wait," said Cora as she closed her eyes to meditate.

***

Grumly climbed up the stone ladder and forced the wooden hatch open and climbed back out in the rain. He closed the hatch and surveyed the area before moving. He had learned that if humans were around and if he sat still long enough, they would ignore him—even if he was perched in the most unlikely place for a gargoyle. He sensed the essence of several small critters nearby, but nothing that would threaten the safety of Cora. He saw the perimeter of a brick wall that looked like the structure of an old house.

Grumly explored the surrounding property in the rain and found what looked like the remains of someone's life that had left in a hurry. He found old roofing tiles and furniture that had fallen apart from the constant rain and moisture. Every so often, Grumly would push aside old wood or bricks to see if anything was hiding under the remains of the old house. He usually found only waterlogged books, broken dishes, and mud-covered clothes. Eventually the gargoyle got bored and sat perched on the crumbling chimney of the fireplace.

***

Kenny missed his exit for work and continued on the highway to the airport. He parked his truck in long-term parking and walked to the terminal. He purchased a one-way ticket on the next flight to the northwest coast of Oregon state.

***

Billy stuffed his backpack full of fruit, breakfast bars, bottles of water, and various other foods. His father, Luke, walked in the kitchen and watched him throw a bag of chips into his backpack.

"What are you doing?" he asked.

Billy turned around in a start. "Oh, hi, Dad."

Luke repeated, "What are you doing?"

"Just grabbing some snacks," Billy said.

Billy pulled his backpack onto his back and tried to walk past his dad. Luke let him walk past but grabbed the backpack and pulled his son back into the kitchen. He unzipped the bag and saw the amount of food he took.

"Are you feeding an army?" he asked.

Billy dropped his head in defeat.

"No, just a friend."

Luke turned his son around. "A friend?" He smirked. "Who?"

"Jamie."

Luke chuckled and tousled his boy's hair and pushed him away. Billy turned and walked out of the kitchen and toward the front door before his father changed his mind. He reached the front door and pulled it open and saw the downpour of rain. He pulled on his boots and the rain poncho over his upper body and backpack. He pulled the hood up and turned around and saw his father standing in the kitchen with his back to him.

Billy said, "Dad, I love you."

He turned and ran out the front door, closing it behind him before his dad could respond.

***

Luke turned around in time to watch the front door close and see his son through the front window running in the rain. He smiled and whispered, "I love you, too."

***

Billy was not surprised to see Grumly perched on the crumbling chimney when he arrived later that afternoon. Grumly silently glided down to the ground and lifted the wooden hatch with ease for Billy.

"Thanks," said Billy as he climbed down the stone ladder into the tunnel.

Grumly closed the hatch and Billy assumed he resumed his sentry duties over the entrance. Billy followed the tunnel until it turned and opened up to the room with the labyrinth. He saw Cora sitting in the middle of the labyrinth cradling Lance. Bozz sat near the tunnel's entrance. He pulled off his backpack and opened the bag. He pulled out two packages of raw steak at the bottom of the bag that his father had missed and handed them both to Bozz.

"One's for Grumly."

The smile on Bozz's face faded as he carried both steaks off into the tunnel to share with Grumly. Billy walked the path of the labyrinth to join Cora and Lance in the center. When he reached the center he sat down next to her and pulled some food and a bottle of water out of his bag and handed it to her.

Billy tried to not watch her chew or drink but he was mesmerized at how beautiful she was. He knew he was too young for her but he enjoyed watching her. He wished someday he could find a woman as equally strong and beautiful as Cora. When he looked away, Lance's body violently jerked. Following a hoarse scream from

Lance's lips, Billy dropped his breakfast bar and pushed himself away on his butt. Cora dropped her water bottle and moved closer to Lance to support his convulsing body.

***

Lance tried to sit up but his body completely failed him. He tried again and again and failed each time. Eventually, two strong hands held him to the ground, and he thought he heard someone speaking, but he could not make out the words. He tried to open his eyes but all he saw were waves of red flashing streaks.

He tried to move again and heard, "Shhhhh, it's okay Lance, relax." Lance did as he was commanded. Not because he was afraid, but because the tone of voice was soothing and healing. His body relaxed and he felt someone brush the hair off of his forehead. Then something pressed to his lips, "Drink this."

Lance parted his lips and he felt water pass over his tongue and into his mouth. He struggled to swallow with his dry throat. When he did the first drink burned. But the next several drinks felt refreshing to his dehydrated body.

***

Kenny stood in front of the sliding glass doors of the Narcolepsy Research Center. The doors were locked because the facility was closed for the night. He saw his reflection with the gold eyes staring back at him and a tall, silver, humanoid creature standing just behind him. Kenny struck the glass doors with his fist and watched his reflection shatter into a million pieces on the ground. He stepped through the frame of the doors and walked into the building.

***

Mark saw the red alarm icon flashing on his computer screen and knew there had to be a problem. He stepped out of his office into the main laboratory and heard the loudest bangs he had ever heard. He turned toward the main door to the laboratory and watched as the wooden door splintered into a half dozen pieces.

"What the hell?" Mark mumbled. He stepped toward the door and paused when a man in plain clothes walked through the splintered door into the laboratory.

With his anger fueling his courage, Mark stepped up to the stranger and pushed him and asked, "What the hell do you think you are doing?"

The man looked at Mark with golden eyes. All of Mark's courage drained from his body. He took a step backward to flee. The stranger with the golden eyes stiff-armed Mark in the chest and sent him flying over a computer console and crashing to the tile floor. Before Mark lost consciousness, he watched as the stranger with the golden eyes ripped the security door off of the chambered vault that housed the body of Gavin Arbitor.

***

Kenny walked into the vault and saw Gavin's body suspended in a pressure-sealed glass case. Without hesitation he walked over and punched his fist through the glass case. The glass shattered and fell to the ground in a pile around Kenny's feet. He stepped closer to the body of Gavin and pried open Gavin's eyes with his fingers.

Kenny's eyes shifted from gold to silver before a silver mist seeped out of his eyes. The silver mist swirled around Kenny's head before encompassing Gavin's head. The silver mist slowly seeped into Gavin's eyes and disappeared. When the silver mist was gone, Kenny's body fell to the ground, lifeless.

***

Gavin rose from his kneeling position above the Valley of Sorrow and watched as the silver Myst floated toward him. Gavin tried to move but was unable to. The Myst stopped in front of him and reached out to grab Gavin's throat. It lifted Gavin off the ground and pinned him to a stone wall that had grown out of the ground above the Valley of Sorrow.

The Myst leaned toward Gavin and whispered, "Your soul will never begin again."

***

Billy pulled the covers over his body and stared up at the ceiling of his bedroom. The images of the past couple days ran through the darkness of his room as he remembered it all. He drifted off to sleep and heard someone enter his room. Sleepy-eyed, he sat up in bed and saw Jamie standing in the doorway of his bedroom. Jamie reached his hand out to his friend.

"Come with me, Billy."

Billy slid out of bed and followed Jamie out of his bedroom and into a field with golden stalks of grass and a purple sky. Not far from where he stood he saw a bluish-green stream flowing through the golden grass. He watched as Jamie threw a stone and it skipped across the water to the other side. Jamie pointed at Billy and then down the stream.

"You want me to follow the stream?" asked Billy.

Jamie nodded yes and faded from Billy's sight. Billy followed the stream and occasionally tried to skip a stone or two across the surface of the water. One stone skipped across the water three times and struck a larger stone on the opposite side. When he focused on the larger stone, he saw a man hanging from the stone.

Billy jumped across the stream and ran up to the man. He parted the man's hair from his face to see if he was still breathing. The man opened his eyes and Billy jumped back in fright.

The man whispered, "Help me."

Billy stepped in closer and brushed his hair away again and could see how tired and beaten he looked. He could see the man was suffering from unbearable pain and it was draining his life's essence.

The man parted his lips again as if wanting to speak. A squeak of sound came from his mouth. Billy stepped closer and faintly heard, "Run"!

Billy backed away and saw a tall silver humanoid creature standing behind the large stone the man hung from. Billy turned on his heels and ran down the hill at full speed. He pumped his arms as fast as his heart pumped and wished his legs would carry him faster.

He reached the stream, leapt across it, and kept running. He glanced back once and saw the silver creature watching him run.

In his mind he heard the man's voice. "Find Lance."

***

Billy awoke on the floor of the hallway when his father tripped over him going to the kitchen. His father caught himself against the wall and danced over Billy to not step on him. Billy looked up at his father and realized he had returned home. In his shorts and T-shirt Billy got up and ran for the front door with his father yelling after him.

"Billy, where the hell are you going?" yelled Luke.

Billy did not stop when he crossed through the front door of the house into the downpour of rain.

***

Lance stood up with the help of Cora, and the image of a silver Myst in a golden field of grass flashed in front of him by one of the torches. The two gargoyles perked up from their slumber as if they had heard something that Lance and Cora could not. Lance grabbed Cora's arm. "Did you see that?" Lance asked.

"See what?"

The image of the Myst in the golden field flashed again and Lance pointed in the direction of the Myst and screamed, "That!"

Cora looked at the wall he pointed at and shook her head no. Bozz moved over toward the section of the wall that Lance had indicated and sniffed around. Grumly moved toward the entrance of the labyrinth chamber as if to stand guard.

The stone floor under Lance and Cora's feet shifted to golden grass, and the torchlight was replaced by the light from a purple sun. Lance looked down at his feet and curled his toes in the golden grass. Cora pushed herself away from Lance and saw the silver Myst standing only a few feet away from them. Then all three of them were back in the labyrinth surrounded by torchlight.

***

Billy ran as fast as he could. He had to keep brushing his wet hair out of his eyes to keep from tripping over mud-covered obstacles. He weaved his way through the trees and bushes to try to reach the remains of the old house before it was too late. He hurdled over the foundation wall and slid to a stop next to the wooden hatch.

He looked around and screamed, "Grumly!"

Nothing.

He dug for the mud-covered wooden hatch and found it. He pulled and struggled until he was able to pry it open. He half-climbed, half-fell down the hole to the stone tunnel.

Grumly caught Billy as he crashed through the hole. He turned and took off flying through the tunnel before Billy knew what was happening. The gargoyle only had to flap its powerful wings a few times to get the speed it needed to travel through the tunnels. Billy saw the end of the tunnel approaching fast and was afraid Grumly was not going to be able to stop. The gargoyle stopped in an instant and released Billy from its arms. Billy instantly ran into the room to find Cora and Lance.

***

Cora turned and watched Billy run dripping wet into the labyrinth chamber. As she looked away, the Myst struck Cora in the back of the head, throwing her to the ground. As she hit the ground Billy slid to a stop. Bozz leapt at the Myst but was struck on the body and hurled against the stone wall like a ball. Lance desperately kicked at the Myst while it was distracted and caught it in the knee. The Myst collapsed to one knee and grabbed Lance's leg, pulling him onto his back. Lance rolled to the side and kicked the Myst in the head with his free leg. The Myst howled and let go of Lance while still trying to claw at him. Lance scrambled to his feet and faced the Myst. The Myst stood to its fullest height with black blood dripping from its face where Lance had kicked it.

The Myst heard Cora trying to scramble to her feet. It kicked her in the side out of frustration. Lance heard Cora's ribs snap when the kick connected. She rolled away toward Billy. Billy grabbed her. He pulled her closer to the wall and away from the fighting. Lance tried to move behind the Myst to strike. The creature backhanded Lance, tossing him against the opposite stone wall. The silver Myst picked up Bozz by his wings and tossed the limp body toward the chamber entrance. Grumly tried to move out of the way but absorbed half of the impact of Bozz as they collided.

***

Billy held on to Cora, preventing her from sitting up. He watched as the silver creature and Lance traded blows. He glanced at Grumly and Bozz as they lay unmoving. He whispered in Cora's ear to try and not draw attention to their position. "Where did he come from?"

"Both worlds must have collided into one," moaned Cora in pain as she tried to move.

Billy grabbed her by the shoulders and gently slid her into the shadows with him. He felt her struggle against him but then she relented and slumped against the wall and Billy's arms.

***

Lance caught the Myst's foot before it struck him in the ribs. He twisted the creature's leg and punched its groin. The Myst fell to the ground. Lance dove on the beast, driving his elbow into its lower back. The Myst threw its head back in pain and Lance grabbed its forehead. Bozz ran back into the labyrinth chamber. The gargoyle kicked the Myst in the jaw, causing Lance to lose his grip. The Myst rolled on his back to reach back and grab the gargoyle. Its dagger fingers dug into the stony flesh of Bozz and threw him against the adjacent wall, knocking him out.

***

Cora broke from Billy's grasp. She half-ran, half-stumbled across the large circular room. When she reached the Myst, she kicked it in the side of the head while it was still on the ground. Its eye ruptured and splattered black blood on the wall. The Myst turned its head to look at Cora with its remaining good eye. She hesitated to look in the alien's last eye before dropping her knee on its jaw and crushing it. The Myst's body tensed in pain and then went limp. She and Lance watched as the alien's body evaporated on the stone floor and a white and silver vapor drifted into the darkness.

"Your soul is free to begin again," they both said in unison.

***

Mark crawled into the vault and watched as Gavin Arbitor's body dissolved into dust.

***

Cora tried to stand up but stumbled back to the ground. Billy raced over to her and caught her. He wrapped his arms around her waist to steady her. She looked down at him and smiled.

Billy blushed.

Lance moved over to Bozz to check on him. He found Grumly nursing Bozz's broken wing. He turned back and joined Cora and Billy. He looked at them both. "Thank you."

Cora let go of Billy and embraced Lance. Lance wrapped his arms around her and held her tight. She whispered in his ear, "Need a place to stay?"

Epilogue

Research Notes of Dr. James Mac

Journal Entry #127 translated from the "wall" text found in the tomb of Gavin Arbitor, circa 1110

I fear our cause is lost. Our fight is in vain. We fight too many foes. We fight against illogical beliefs forced upon us by religious leaders who are corrupt. We fight against a humanity that fears heretics. We fight against our own brothers who seek to halt our battle for liberation. We fight against the Myst that never perish.

Similar to all God's creatures, the Myst are blessed with reincarnation. A reincarnation that our humanity does not fathom. A reincarnation linked to their physical presence. How do we achieve liberation from such great odds?

I look to the heavens for answers and see only one possibility. Perhaps destruction of their corporeal form? But how do we achieve such a lofty endeavor when we must be forced to travel to their celestial abode in the night sky above?

Acknowledgments

Where does one begin to thank all of the individuals who have been part of the writing of this book?

The obvious are my parents, Carol and Ernest, for allowing me to dream and live in a world of fantasy and make-believe, while keeping me firmly rooted in the soil. To my children, Christian and Cassandra, for listening to my stories, enduring my fantastical theories and ideas of how our world works, and snuggling with me when the times were dark. To my long-time friend Bruce Panneton, who read the very first draft of this story so many years ago and gave me his honest feedback. He may not remember, but I do. His candor and straightforward comments strengthened the bones of this tale.

To James Crewe, Editor-in-Chief of Zharmae Publishing, for giving me a chance to live and experience a dream I've held in my heart since I was a boy. To my two wonderful editors, Erin Ormsby and Keri Phillips, for finding a way to pull out details of the story and characters that I didn't know were still inside of me. Thank you to the entire Zharmae crew and artists for their eye to detail, professionalism, and most importantly for bringing my characters to life that have lived for so long in my head. A big thank-you to Laura Taylor and my niece Paige Doyle for trekking into the middle of the woods to take my "author" photo.

And most importantly, thank you to Christine, my Muse, for believing in me and never giving up on me in so many ways. Thank you for giving me the time to write. Thank you for thinking it is cool that I try to write every day. Thank you for sitting on the rocks, or in the woods, or in our living room listening to me read my stories. Thank you for believing with me that my characters and their lives become real when I share them with you. You inspire me. You encourage me. I believe your positive energy and belief in me is why God has blessed me with this adventure.

About the Author

Ernest Solar has been a writer, storyteller, and explorer of some kind for his entire life. He grew up devouring comic books, novels, and any other type of book, along with movies, which allowed him to explore a multitude of universes packed with mystery and adventure. A professor at Mount St. Mary's University in Maryland, he lives with his wife and family in Lovettsville, Virginia.

Credits

Erin Ormsby &Keri Phillips | *Editors*
Jed Tarkovsky | *Artist*
Star Foos | *Designer*
Benjamin Grundy | *Typesetter*
Rachel Garcia | *Reader*
Cindy Crumrine | *Copy Editor*
Jim Walker | *Proofreader*
Amanda Smith | *Copy Writer & Reviewer*
Edward Mack | *Coordinating Producer*
Erin Sinclair | *Managing Editor*
Shannon Godwin | *Associate Publisher*
Travis Robert Grundy | *Publisher*
August 2015 | *The Zharmae Publishing Press*